I0628130

Fast-paced science fiction, humor and a journey into the world of rock and roll.

Mark Gutstein was a typical young man of 1996. Calm, relatively anonymous, one more number in the files of the government.

Then his best friend is murdered, leaving a strange set of clues to the secret of the crime.

It is a puzzle so incredible that Gutstein is forced to solve it himself—

—but to do it he had to travel time and that, of course, was impossible—wasn't if?

A spectacular Illustrated fantasy!

other books from
Byron Preiss Visual Publications

I—ALIEN
by J. Michael Reaves
Illustrated by Terry Austin

THE ILLUSTRATED ROGER ZELAZNY
by Roger Zelazny
Illustrated by Gray Morrow

THE ILLUSTRATED HARLAN ELLISON
by Harlan Ellison
Illustrated by Steranko, Reese,
Sutton, McLoughlin, Dillon,
Stout and Loyd

story by
Byron Preiss
additional text by
C.J. Henderson
illustrations by
Gray Morrow
frontispiece designed by Michael Golden

J. T. Colby & Company, Inc.
Purveyors of
Time Travel Instruments
and Accessories™

iBooks
Manhanset House
Dering Harbor, New York 11965

bricktower@aol.com • www.ibooksinc.com

All rights reserved under the International and Pan-American
Copyright Conventions. No part of this publication may be reproduced, stored
in a retrieval system, or transmitted in any form or by any means, electronic,
or otherwise, without the prior written permission of the copyright holder. The
iBooks colophon is a trademark of J. Boylston & Company, Publishers.

GUTS

Copyright © 1979 by Byron Preiss Visual Publications, Inc.
Illustrations ©1979 by Byron Preiss Visual Publications, Inc.
All Rights Reserved
ISBN: 978-1-59687-950-8

January 2021

Cover painting by Gray Morrow based on
a pencil illustration by Michael Golden

Interior logo by Alex Jay

The author wishes to thank Joan Brandt, Shirley Feldman, Alex Jay, Gray
Morrow and Robin London for their help with the extreme time and deadline
problems related to this series.

Prologue

What is time?

What is an hour, a minute, or even a day? Sometimes an hour seems like a day. Sometimes a minute seems like an hour. The thirty minutes you spend taking a math test may seem far longer than the thirty minutes you spend eating ice cream, pizza, and french fries. Yet it is exactly the same length of time.

Time can get you in trouble. Sometimes there doesn't seem to be enough of it. You plan to take a bath, play your new Neil Diamond cassette, do some work, and meet four friends for lunch, but suddenly, it's three in the afternoon. *Where did the time go?*

Yet time can also help you. You're supposed to meet your best friend at *5:30* but it's only *3:30,* and you have nothing to do for two hours, and then you see this terrific looking person sitting near you in the library, and—*you get the picture?*

Did you ever think what life would be like without time? No hours, no minutes, no months? Suddenly things would happen at once. Or nothing would happen at all. You think it's 1979 and suddenly it's 1956.

Could you handle it? Or would it drive you crazy?

Would you be able to do what you are doing now or would you go insane just thinking about all the problems?

Do you wear a watch? Two hands, correct? Or maybe you have a digital. *Four numbers?* When it runs down, you reset it, correct? You change your watch to show the proper time of day.

What if things were reversed? What if the time of day changed when you turned the handle on your watch? What if you could use it to travel time? What if you could turn months and years back to 1278 or 1806? Where would you go? What would you do if you knew you might not be able to come back? Would you stay here with your family and friends or would you take a chance?

Would you be a hero or a fool? Alive or dead? Would you love the past or would it scare you? Would you like things better without TV and cars? Or would you run around 1776 screaming for a shake and fries?

Have a look at that watch of yours again. Does it have a little window on it that tells you the year? No? Then look at a calendar. No, not that calendar! You should be looking at the calendar for *1996*. That's where we're headed. This book is your time machine. Return trip guaranteed.

—Unless, of course, your name is Mark Gutstein. Then, my friend, you are in trouble. Oh, boy, are you in trouble.

CHAPTER ONE

It was July 17, 1996. It was the fifty-seventh birthday of the rock musician Spencer Davis and the thirty-seventh anniversary of the legendary blues singer Billy Holiday's death.

To Mark Gutstein it was just another day.

It was summer and Mark had just finished his last level of high school. Although he had enjoyed vacation, he was already looking forward to attending college in September with his best friend, Herbie Bender. Herbie had started two years before him, even though they were both the same age. As the teachers in their high school used to say, "Herbie was exceptional."

Mark was late for a meeting with Herbie. He had rushed into the glass elevator of his apartment building and was now running down a landscaped walkway in a town called Mega.

When Mark was a baby, the government had bulldozed much of an old New Jersey town named Elizabeth. The action was part of a Federal Environment Renaissance program. On the site of Elizabeth, the town of Mega had been built. Where once had been a heavily polluted city, the federally-funded state-managed crews had erected twenty long, low-rise structures made of stone, chrome, and glass. The new town featured rolling hills and shrubs. The twenty community buildings shared the same medical, social, commercial, educational, and recreational facilities. Mark had been content living in Mega. Food, entertainment, and recreation were always within walking distance. As they sang on holovision, "You never have to leave."

That same jingle came to Mark's ear as he passed a dark-haired girl with a portable radio. She smiled shyly at him in an appealing way. She hoped he would follow her, but hadn't the faintest idea of what she would do if he did.

Mark eyed her. "Too young," was his thought, and he continued on his way to Herbie's apartment. As he jogged, he imagined the upcoming conversation with Herbie.

"What happened, Mark? Blond or brunette?"

"Sorry, Herbie. I just. . . ."

"You just don't think about the time!"

"I'm sorry."

"Don't always apologize, Mark. Look at a clock! They're all over Mega!" Then Herbie would frown, as if "Mega" was a bad word or something. That was Herbie. Prompt, smart, and a talker. He'd find something to say about everything—even holovision jingles like "You never have to leave."

"They never want you to leave, is more like it," Herbie would say.

Mark would frown. He didn't always understand Herbie. All of Mark's friends liked Mega. He looked forward to coming back to the town after college. What did Herbie have against it? Why did he always stay indoors? Why was he always taking the monorail into the city of Philadelphia? College was out on vacation, too!

Maybe I can get Herbie down to the Youth Center today, Mark thought. If I could just get him away from his old records for a day, maybe he could meet some girls. Or shoot some baskets. If I have to listen to another lecture about rock and roll or physics or Philadelphia, I'll be doin' loonie-flips.

Wrapped up in his thoughts about Herbie, Mark stepped onto a blue walkway. Mega was surrounded by three travel-ways. Each was color-coded. The blue was for the handicapped, and for pedestrians in general. The green was for recreation, street sports, joggers, etc. The red, slightly removed from the other two, was reserved for Mega's small electric vehicles and bicycles. Not many vehicles dotted the redway. Energy consumers like gas-burning cars and motorcycles had been banned. Even electric cars required a valid reason for ownership. The town had been planned for

pedestrian traffic. To reach Philly and other cities, there was a monorail, subsidized by the state's taxes, and accessible by foot. Who needed a car? As the saying went, "In Mega, we do the planning and leave the leisure time to you." That was another jingle-phrase Herbie didn't like.

Mark hurried down the blueway. In the distance was Mega Building 20, and, surprise of surprises, Herbie was waiting outside!

"Late again," he said as Mark approached.

"I know!" Mark shouted. "I got a flat tire!"

Herbie laughed. It was a private joke between them. Neither friend owned a bike; they walked everywhere.

"All right," said Herbie. "Hurry up! I told Mazzari and Wein we'd meet them at the Youth Center."

Mark was surprised again. "The Youth Center? You told them to meet you at the *Center?* You can't stand the Center, Herbie! You always tell me it's full of garbageheads."

Herbie seemed edgy. He didn't answer with his usual wit. "We're late," he said, and Mark wondered why he was moving so quickly to get to a place he enjoyed so little.

Mazzari and Wein were waiting outside the Youth Center. Mazzari, tall, skinny and gushing with acne, held a small blue box under his arm. Wein, on his left, stood silently, a half-eaten slice of pizza in his hand. Upon spotting Mark and Herbie, Mazzari started to smile.

"Hey, Guts! Have I got something for you!" Mazzari waved the blue box in the air. "You gotta hear this back-stacked viddisc!"

" 'Lo, Herbie," said Wein.

Mazzari enthusiastically slipped a small black circle from his hand into the blue box. It was a viddisc player, capable of emitting both sound and picture simultaneously. A laser beam decoded both music and visual material from microscopic bumps on the surface of the black disc. A tiny speaker and screen were built into the box. Mazzari and Wein watched it intently, and as the laser activated, a song started to play.

"You gotta hear this!" said Mazzari.

"Uh," said Wein. He looked sleepy.

Mark nodded and listened to the music.

A snare drum started the beat. Four electric guitars joined it, followed by random patterns played suggestively on two organs. As the four youths listened, the instruments tightened, the rhythm became faster, sharper. Mark and Mazzari took turns looking at the blue portapack, on which a picture of the musicians appeared. As always, they were in shadow. There were numerous colors and patterns behind them. It didn't matter. It was the music that was important, not the faces. The viddisc's sound was having its usual effect. The kids were caught in its spell. The disc ran nearly four minutes, but only Herbie noticed. The other three were oblivious. It could have been ten. They kept pace with the rhythm, as if it were a call to the stars. "The future's in the music," said a holovision ad, and nobody argued. They listened to the disc, from one end to the other, flipped it over, and continued. Nothing distracted them. They thought the music was beautiful. It was called synthenization.

"Fantastic, huh Guts?" said Mazzari.

"I'm impressed," said Wein, and he dropped his slice of pizza as he continued to tap his foot on the ground.

"He's stoned," Herbie whispered to Mark.

Mazzari, embarrassed for his friend, said, "Wein, the song's over now!"

Wein did not respond at first. Then he blinked, and saw the three friends watching him. "Ahhh!" he said, "you guys just don't know how to have fun." He started to turn away, realized one foot was covered by the pizza, turned red, slid six inches so that the pizza would fall off his shoe, then shifted into a run.

"I have to talk to that boy," said Mazzari.

"Stoned?" asked Mark.

"No," said Mazzari, "I was with him all morning. He's been that way on and off lately. It bothers me."

Mark nodded sympathetically, and then said, "It was a nice song."

"Nice?" said Mazzari. "It was *spectaculous!*"

Herbie smiled. "It was spectaculous — for an old song."

Mark looked at his friend. *Not again!* he thought, *Herbie, don't get into a fight about music again!*

Mazzari sighed. He had already taken the bait. "What do you mean, an old song, Herbie? The Quantum Leap is a new group. The song just came out last week!"

"I know," said Herbie, "but that's not the first time. That song is about forty years old."

Mazzari was not known for patience. "Guts," he said, "tell this jelly roll that synthenization isn't even fifteen years old! There is no way this tune could be forty years old!"

Herbie shook his head. "The song is 'You Send Me.' It's by Sam Cooke."

Mazzari put the blue box down on a nearby ledge. "You're senile, Herbie."

"No, I'm not. That song was done by Sam Cooke. C-O-O-K-E. *Cooke.*"

Mazzari calmly opened the lid of the viddisc player and took out the record. "Look at the label code, you loonie-flip. See what it says. *'216'* by *'Quantum Leap.'* Not *Sam Cookie.*"

Herbie sighed. "The singer's name was Sam Cooke. The original version was called 'You Send Me.' Forget what your viddisc reads, Mazzari. It only came out last week. I have a record in my roon from 1957, and it's the same song. It was by Sam Cooke!"

"1957? Herbie, there wasn't even synthenization in 1957! Just museum stuff—old rock and roll! The Quantum Leap commercials are all over holovision! You think they'd spend that sort of money on imitations? Are you crazy? Herbie, I know you're smart, but this time you've got things confused!"

"Confused? Mazzari, don't you see? Holovision's getting to your mind just like these viddiscs! It's not the truth! They make them to sell things to you, not to teach you!"

"Are you calling the holovision commercials liars?" Mazzari was ready for action. "Are you saying *Quantum Leap* is a fake?"

"Cool it!" said Mark. "It's only a song."

"You tell Herbie to cool it," said Mazzari. "He likes to make other people look like idiots. I'm not stupid, Herbie. I watch as much holovision as anybody, and I know more about synthenization than you do. Don't tell me about music!"

Herbie spoke softly. "I don't think you're stupid, Mazzari. I'm just looking to explain something. That song was a hit in 1957.

They released it on vinyl records back then—they didn't have lasers."

"They musta had lasers in 1957," said Mazzari with less confidence.

"No, they didn't. People used little metal needles to listen to songs on boxes called phonographs. 'You Send Me' sold more little phonograph records than any other for a while. It was called the Number One record in the country. It was one of the early hits of rock and roll!"

"Maybe," said Mazzari, "but what does that have to do with Quantum Leap's viddisc? Rock and roll was a million years ago!"

"It was only forty years ago. Your day probably heard Sam Cooke's records when he was really young."

"If it's that old, than you're definitely confused, Herbie. How could it have anything to do with synthenization?"

Herbie was excited, but not angry. "It does, Mazzari! It does!" He smiled. "Get this. Sam Cooke started off as a gospel singer. Then he sang a type of music called rhythm and blues. The way he sang rhythm and blues was influenced by the way he had sung gospel. He was so appealing in the way he sang rhythm and blues that his records affected another type of music—rock and roll."

Mazzari looked puzzled.

"Don't you see," said Herbie. "Music affects music! Gospel affected rhythm and blues! Rhythm and blues affected rock and roll, and rock and roll. . . ."

"Affected synthenization?" said Mark, having heard the lecture many times in the past.

"Yes!" said Herbie. "Do you understand, Mazzari?"

Mazzari nodded. "You're saying Quantum Leap stole 'You Send Me' from a rock and roll singer named Sam Cooke."

"No!" said Herbie. "They didn't steal it! They were affected by it. They liked the sound and they wanted to hear it in terms of their own approach to music."

Mark felt relieved. It was the conclusion of the speech. He didn't understand why Herbie got so excited. Music was music—what was the difference who sang it?

Mazzari closed the lid of his viddisc player and looked toward the front of the Youth Center. "That's very interesting, Herbie," he said. "See y' around the Center."

Herbie and Mark watched him leave.

"You did it again," said Mark. "You make Mazzari feel stupid."

"I had to explain it, Mark. You just don't understand."

"Now *I* don't understand? Herbie, you're really looking to lose all your friends."

"Mark! Really, you have to trust me! There are a lotta things I've learned. . . ."

"Herbie, I *know* you're smart. You don't have to prove it to me."

Herbie put his hand on Mark's shoulder. "Look, you're my best friend. I need you now, Mark. I need you to trust me. Come back to my room. I'll play you the original record. Then you can tell me if I'm crazy."

Mark looked at Herbie. He was nervous but that wasn't unusual for Herbie. Yet he was more than nervous. Herbie seemed scared.

"Sure I'll visit," he said to Herbie. Something's bothering him, thought Mark. He's holding it back. Maybe he'll talk inside his apartment.

The two friends turned away from the Center and hurried down the blue track to Mega-20, where Herbie had rented a small apartment for summer vacation.

CHAPTER TWO

"You're fortunate to have this place while your folks are on vacation." Mark sat back in an old easy chair, waiting for Herbie to find the record of "You Send Me." If it hadn't been filed in order, it would have taken all day. The largest wall of the bedroom was covered with shelves, all of them packed with albums and singles from thirty, forty, and fifty years in the past. Herbie rummaged for a moment on the "C" area of a lower shelf. A minute later, he pulled a square cardboard jacket in a plastic bag away from the others.

"This is it," said Herbie. "Actually, this isn't the original. They released this collection after Sam Cooke had made the little record of 'You Send Me.' They called these things lp's."

Mark smiled. "This is supposed to be such a big classic and all, and you don't have the original? Herbie Bender, scholar of rock and roll?"

"I have a copy, Mark. It's just hard to find the 45's."

"The what?"

"They called the little records 45's. Or singles. Forty-five was the number of times the record turned per minute. Forty-five revolutions per minute, forty-five rpm. I have a copy of the 45 record here, but it's harder to find since there's no label on the spine. It's in my log book."

Mark nodded. "The log book you never let me see."

Herbie turned his back to Mark and reached into a drawer of his desk.

"What are you doing?"

Herbie turned around again and in his hand was a large black book. "I think it's about time," he said.

Mark was shocked. Herbie had always been secretive about the ledger. Although Mark was his best friend, even he had been unable to get a peek at Herbie's secret log book. Now, all of a sudden, Herbie had pulled it out from his desk. Something was up. Herbie was nervous. It was unlike him to be casual about a treasured book.

"I don't want to see this if you don't want me to see it," said Mark.

"Look at it," said Herbie, and he turned on the antique stereo. A small diamond-tipped needle dropped to a groove on the shiny disc. A harsh crackle of static came onto the speakers at the other end of the room. Mark looked up. Herbie was tapping his foot. Try as he might, Mark could never get used to the scratching, buzzing scrape which accompanied so many of Herbie's old records. Viddisc rarely had any noise. He set the log book on the small table next to the stereo as the song started to play.

Herbie watched Mark as they both listened to the sound coming from the speakers. He wanted to see if Mark could recognize the song. He did. It was unavoidable. If you took away the usual overbeat, changed the instruments, got rid of the electronics, and slowed the beat down, it was the same song.

The underlying pattern, the style, the heart of the tune was in this version, sung more than a decade before either of them had been born.

"What's your opinion, Mark?"

"That's the same song as '216,' Herbie."

"Thanks."

"That Sam Cooke was some singer."

"I'm glad you appreciate it, Mark. It's not synthenization. You know, I always thought you should study music. You have an exceptional understanding of the form for an occasional listener."

"Thanks, Herbie, but that's not what it said in my aptitude tests."

"Damn the tests," said Herbie. That was another of his complaints. All testing in Mega was counter-productive, Herbie had argued. Mark did not understand what that meant.

Mark looked at his friend. He was biting a nail. "Herbie, what's bugging you?"

The young man turned red. "Bugging me? Nothing. It's just these viddisc corporations—they keep releasing one song after another based on the old stuff and never give anybody credit. Mark, I know we've had this talk before, but synthenization is garbage, it's terrible. . . ."

"C'mon, Herbie, not all of it is garbage!"

"Too much of it!" Herbie sat down on the bed next to his friend. "Mark, the stuff is dangerous. You just don't know what I know."

Herbie was shuddering.

"Herbie, I'm your friend, you can tell me."

"No, I can't."

"Nothing can be that bad. You have a crush on some girl in Philly?"

Herbie rubbed his cheek. "No, no girls, no personal problem. Just forget I said anything. Look at the log book for a while. I have some other new songs I think you'll like here. I got them on my last trip to the city."

The pair sat for a while, Herbie playing different records for Mark, both listening and commenting on the music. After a couple of hours, however, Mark knew that it was time to head home.

"I'll drop back and see you after dinner," he said.

"I'll be here." Herbie took the log book from the bed and returned it to his desk drawer. He seemed more relaxed now.

As Mark walked to the elevator he smiled as he thought of Herbie. Always blowing things out of proportion, always arguing. He couldn't remember a time when his friend hadn't made a fuss about something.

"There's something else," he whispered to himself, "but Herbie's hiding it." Mark hurried down the blue track toward his parents' apartment, the windows of Mega-20 reflecting the afternoon sun behind him.

"How's Herbie doing these days, son?" asked Mark's father, as he scooped potatoes onto his plate.

"He's all right."

"Does he still collect those old records?"

"He has enough to open a store."

His father liked Herbie. He respected his taste in music. "I'd like to listen to some of his stuff. Ray Charles, Jerry Lee Lewis, and Chuck Berry—and Dylan, I'll bet he has a lot of Dylan records, doesn't he?"

"Yeah, he played me a couple of Dylan tunes once." "Boy, those were the days, back when music was still good, not this junk they play now." As his dad started one of his typical "I remember" spiels, Mark tuned him out, finishing his dinner with "um-humms."

After dinner, Mark and his parents went into the living room of their apartment. It was small, as were all the rooms in all the apartments of Mega, but it had a large window for one wall and a four-foot holovision screen on another. Mark's mother sat in a large plastic chair facing the holovision screen and pressed a toggle switch on the wall behind her. The screen lit up and filled the room with a swirl of color as the picture came into focus.

"Can't we just talk?" asked Mark's father.

"Sh," said his mother, "there's something on this evening that I want Mark to see."

She pushed a button next to the toggle switch and there was the familiar blur of the screen as ninety-eight channels of active broadcasting changed. A small monitor next to the screen indicated the channels by numbers and letters. When 68 had passed, Mark's mother took her hand off the switch.

"Channel 70?" asked Mark. "There's never anything interesting on Channel 70."

"There is tonight," she answered.

A blue and white title came up on the screen. It said, "The State of Israel."

"Mom," whined Mark.

"Be quiet and listen," said his father.

The hologram was quite beautiful. It was a travelogue with biblical references, explaining many of the sights in the Jewish state.

"Can I leave now?" Mark asked after twenty minutes of the show.

"Not until it's over, son," said his mother, who continued to watch attentively.

Mark felt uncomfortable. He was Jewish, and he knew he was supposed to be interested in this travelogue about Israel, but he did not know why. Herbie was also Jewish, but he had been taught many things that Mark hadn't. Mark remembered Herbie's Bar Mitzvah in Philadelphia, a ceremony at the time of a Jewish boy's thirteenth birthday, after which he takes on the moral responsibilities of a man. He had always wondered why his parents hadn't arranged the same ceremony for him. He didn't know why his father and mother wanted him to watch the HV show. They were doing a lot of things like that these days. Like putting on radio shows about Jewish holidays when they occurred.

If they wanted to learn something, why didn't they just tell him?

He asked Herbie about it a few days ago on the phone.

"Maybe they don't know a lot about the holidays themselves," Herbie had said.

"Then why don't they learn?" Mark had answered.

"I don't know. They should. Why don't you ask them?"

Mark had never asked his folks. He wanted to ask them now, he wanted to learn more about his heritage, but he was embarrassed to ask. He didn't know why.

He sat there, watching the beautiful travelogue about Israel, but did not talk.

Then a special alert appeared on the screen. It was a black-and-white broadcast by local equipment. That meant it had to do with Mega.

Mark looked at his parents. They seemed worried. All three waited for an announcement.

CHAPTER THREE

THIS IS A SPECIAL PUBLIC SERVICE BULLETIN OF THE MEGA BROADCASTING SERVICE.

The color of the holovision screen was deep orange. This meant that something dangerous had occurred within Mega city limits. With an abrupt swirl, the color transformed into the features of the station's news anchorman.

"This is Bob Lantel with a Mega newsflash. All Mega citizens are cautioned to stay off the blue, green, and redways. There has been an explosion in Mega-20. Security officials are investigating now."

"Mega-20! Dad, that's where Herbie lives!"

"Word of the blast, which seems to have caused little damage, reached our studios just moments ago from the central regulatory offices of the mayor. She requests that those citizens who do not need to leave their homes at this time do not do so. Security forces have cleared the area. Until the cause of the explosion is determined, there is concern that more blasts of the same nature may occur. A team of Federal Special Forces men is already investigating the explosion site. At this moment, no terrorist organization has claimed the credit for what can only be termed a senseless act. An unconfirmed source says that dangerous equipment, the personal property of the ruined apartment's occupant, may be responsible for the explosion."

The newscaster himself looked nervous. Such things did not happen in Mega.

Mark stood up anxiously and headed toward the door.

"Son, where are you going?"

"Dad, Mega-20 was Herbie's building."

"Mark, you heard what they said. No one is supposed to go into that area! You'll just be in the way."

"But dad, Herbie might have been hurt. I'm slipping out. I have to find out!"

"You'll stay right here, Mark. The HV told everybody to stay inside. You couldn't get near the place, they're clearing the area. You'd just add to the confusion." Mark's father sighed. "Son, Mega-20 is a big building. You don't know that it was Herbie's apartment. Now just wait to hear what else the announcer has to say."

The HV screen had continued to spew time-wasting filler information. Mark was impatient. He wanted to get over there and find out for himself. Finally, the pattern of color swirled again and location shots of Mega-20 appeared on the HV screen.

"This is the outer wall of Mega-20, where the explosion took place. Our mobile transmitters are still not being allowed any closer."

Mr. Gutstein stared intently at the HV image. Even at the distance the hologram was being taken from, he could tell the outer wall being shown was badly burned. He also knew who lived close by. He had walked past Mega-20 often enough with Mark to know the sector in which Herbie's apartment was located.

"That clinches it," said Mark. "I'm off!"

* * *

Most of the smoke had been dissipated by the wind by the time Mark arrived. There was no hole in the outer wall, but scorching and a large crack identified the area of the explosion. Chips of cement and plaster littered the lawn in a semicircle reaching almost to the walkway. The lucite window, although it had not shattered, had cracked in several places and was now darkened by soot.

What could Herbie have had in there? thought Mark as he ran up to the edge of the security perimeter. *It does look like a bomb exploded!*

As he neared the blockade, a friendly security man waved him to a stop. "Sorry, son. You can't go in there."

"I've gotta get to somebody!"

"It can wait a minute or two, can't it? This area isn't safe. At least, it hasn't been declared so, yet. You can't have anything that important to do in there."

"I have to see the apartment that was blown up!"

"Why?"

"My friend lived there," said Mark innocently. "My best friend lived in there! I have to make sure he's not hurt."

"If he is, they'll be bringing him out any minute. Calm down now, son. He'll be all right. You'll see."

"What could have done it?" Mark glanced again at the wall.

"You mean the blast? I don't know. I can't think of anything in the building. It's possible for main energy circuits to severely overload, but if they did, more of Mega would have been damaged."

"Then how'd it happen?"

"I couldn't tell you. Your friend must have had some kind of explosives in his room." The security man was growing impatient.

"Not Herbie!" Mark answered, but he realized that he didn't really know what Herbie may have hidden in there. "Look, couldn't I just have a look?"

"I'm sorry, son. I have my orders. 'Course you could ask Captain Gruder. But," the guard looked about, "I don't see him anywhere. Please wait. Your friend will be all right. Just wait and you'll see for yourself."

Mark slowly walked away. Milling with the crowd, he stared at the building, waiting for something to happen. Something troubled him. Something in the picture was out of place, but he could not give it a name. Everything seemed normal, but something bothered him about it nevertheless. He realized the security men had to keep people back from the blast area. Until they knew what had caused the explosion, they could not take the chance that there might not be another. He understood, but he wanted to know what had happened to Herbie! The announcer on the HV had said it might be personal equipment of the owner that caused the explosion. Maybe this meant

Herbie's electronic equipment . . . but Herbie had told Mark that all of the machinery he had brought to the apartment was safe! Good old Herbie had taken an *entire* Sunday afternoon to explain how safe it all was, but, if so, then what had caused the explosion? Why had Herbie seemed so troubled earlier? Mark returned to the same question. *What had happened to Herbie?*

Then he saw it. He was almost surprised that he even noticed. He realized what was troubling him. The government Special Forces people were there! All right, the HV *had* said they were investigating, but there were too many of them. For every Mega local security officer, he could count two federal men. Their caramel and black uniforms could be spotted all around Mega-20. How could so many have gotten on the scene so fast?

They couldn't have been watching Herbie, thought Mark. He's just a college kid!

He searched the crowd for anything else that might look suspicious. He'd learned in *Special Studies* that the nearest federal office was in Philadelphia. If that was correct, then there was no way, even by monorail express, for the men to get here so fast. As he watched the people, he spotted the Mega security man he had talked to only minutes ago. The officer was now talking to a federal man. As they continued to talk, the federal man seemed to grow angry. As Mark watched, the federal agent took off his helmet and eyed the crowd. Mark stepped quickly behind an older man. He did not know why, but he had a feeling the government man was looking for him. He realized he was being foolish, but he knew he did not want to be found.

Mark knew that he would have to get into Herbie's apartment to learn anything. The police would not tell him. The federal agent made him very nervous. He would have to play detective, like in one of the old video shows on HV. Circling around to the other side of Mega-20, he rang the bell of one of his friends.

"Who's there?"

"Stevie, it's Mark."

"What do you want?" came a shout. "I'm watching the HV!"

"Open up, Stevie!"

A few minutes later, the door slid open. Mark stepped into the foyer. As usual, Stevie was still seated in the back room watching the big HV screen. Mark slipped through the apartment, rushing toward the hallway door on the other side. He pushed a wall button and the door whirled back. A minute later, Mark was waiting at the elevators of Mega-20.

Mark took the first car to the fourth floor. It would take ten minutes to walk around to the other side of the complex where the explosion had occurred. Mark jogged the distance. The explosion still made no sense to him. The more he thought about the situation, the *less* sense it seemed to make. He was worried about Herbie—and himself. He had gone against official orders, and if they would not let him into Herbie's building, how was he to get into Herbie's own apartment?

As he reached a familiar hallway on Herbie's side of Mega-20, Mark spied a Federal Special Forces man. He kept walking forward, trying not to let his nervousness show.

He had always been taught to think that the government was on his side. They were good. He had no reason to be feeling the way he did, but he could not shake the feelings inside him. Something had happened to Herbie. Something was about to happen to him.

As he came closer to the apartment, Mark realized the federal man had been watching him. So, as the federal man approached, Mark simply asked, "Hey, you're a Special Forces agent, aren't you?"

Caught by surprise with the question, the man replied, "Yes I am. Can I help you?"

Mark steadied himself. Herbie always said he could be clever when he took the time to think. Boy, was he thinking now! He remembered the name of the Special Forces agent mentioned by the local officer outside Mega-20 and said, "A guy named Gruder told me to tell the Special Forces man up here to go downstairs."

"*Captain* Gruder . . . ?" asked the federal man.

"I dunno if he was a captain. I just know what he told me to do. Listen. I can't stand here and argue all night. I got to get home for supper."

Mark started to walk away. He hoped the guard would leave, but he did not dare look back. As he rounded the corner from the apartment, however, he heard the bell tone which indicated that an elevator had arrived. Mark heard the doors open in the hallway. He looked around the corner cautiously and saw that the guard had entered the elevator.

"Terrific!" he whispered to himself.

Then, as the door slid shut, he raced back toward Herbie's apartment. The front door was still open. He quickly stepped inside and headed for the bedroom, where the explosion had obviously taken place. As he stared through the darkness at the damage, he suddenly heard voices. There was somebody in the kitchen! Before Mark could think of anything to do, the phone chimed. An officer named Munroe came out of the kitchen and depressed a button, activating the phone and its speaker.

"Apartment R15," he said nervously. "Who is calling?"

"It's just me, chief," came a voice from the speaker. "I just got a call from Donaldson! He wants to know what you've found!"

"Tell him I'll file when I get back to the city."

"He sounds anxious, chief. You know Donaldson." The man named Munroe nodded. "I've known Donaldson for a long time. He wants me to take the rap for this disaster. I know his tricks."

"He has clout, chief."

"He wants to pin Bender on me."

"I have to call him back, chief."

"All right. Now listen. Tell Donaldson the phone must have been ruined in the explosion because you couldn't get through. Tell him you called the ground forces, but they were undermanned and couldn't send a man up. How's that scan?"

"He won't like it."

"Go tell him the news. I've got to get back trying to salvage something from this mess."

Munroe deactivated the phone. Another man was busy searching the bathroom. Mark felt his heart jump through his chest. He had to get out of there! He heard Munroe say, "All right, we have to finish up. Bob, rip that phone out. Donaldson is sure to call to check it out for himself . . . Jones, you come with me."

There were two more of them. Mark quickly surveyed the ruins of Herbie's apartment. Luckily for Mark, the government men had gone through it first and were already finished. The room was in a shambles. The record shelves had been demolished.

Bits of plastic, broken and melted, were strewn about the room. He had hoped to find some clue as to what had happened to Herbie, to what had caused the explosion, but faced with the debris in front of him, he realized that he did not even know what he was looking for in the apartment. Nonetheless, he knew there must be something there that could help him, something that Herbie could . . . *the log book!*

He remembered the lengths to which Herbie had gone to show it to him. He scrambled through the debris, searching, scavenging, for the black cloth cover. Minutes later, he found it, hidden under a pile of records. It lay face-down on the floor, as if one of the agents had examined it and then tossed it aside. He picked it up. He found everything intact, the slips of paper, all the pages of numbers and song titles, and the old record in the back. Mark grabbed up some other papers from a chair, stuffing them in his shirt around the log book for protection. He thought about searching for anything else that looked like a clue, but then he heard the voices again. Cautiously, he peered around the corner. The captain was gone, but two of his men were in the foyer drinking coffee. He kept watching, praying that they would go into the back room, or the kitchen. As the seconds dragged by, beads of perspiration rolled down Mark's face. His hands were covered with soot from the ruins of the explosion. As he wiped at his forehead, streaks of grime were left on his face. He could feel them. He tried to calmly wipe the smears away with his sleeve, but as he raised his arm, the papers in his shirt began to rustle. He froze. He put his arm down slowly, ignoring the irritating sweat which was soaking his face, stinging his eyes.

He already had quite a load of evidence, none of which he understood. He thought he might find a clue as to what had caused the explosion in the things he had taken. To his surprise, however, an answer came quickly from the voices in the next room.

"So why don't we take what we have and leave?"

"It's not that easy, Ralph," said the man named Bob. "Even with the problems, it still comes off like an accident. That's how it's supposed to be. This thing has been planned for weeks. We do everything by the book."

23

Mark was confused. The conversation the two men were having made things sound as if *they* had planned Herbie's accident. If they did, if the federal government was framing Herbie, then it had to be something big. That was crazy! Why in the world would they want a kid like Herbie? Why would they consider....

Mark was scared. The evidence, the discussion between the agents, suggested that Herbie had been murdered. The government had murdered Herbie!

That made no sense at all! The government was good. Wasn't it? Why would they hurt anybody from Mega?

Mark was dripping wet. He had to get out of the apartment, out of Mega-20. He had to think about everything he had learned. Maybe he was exaggerating. Maybe there was another answer.

He watched the news, he watched HV. He watched HV *every* day. It would tell him the truth; it relayed news as soon as it happened. If the government was up to something, HV would tell the people. Wouldn't it?

Before Mark could think of an answer, he heard the two men in the room outside. They were heading into the kitchen with their coffee cups.

He had to get out, now! Quietly, he stepped out of the bedroom. In another few steps, he would be out the door. Bracing himself, he took the last three steps and prepared for the flight through the hallway. He took a deep breath, looked out toward the fourth floor elevators and ran!

"Hold it!"

Mark glanced at the last elevator in the hall.

Coming toward him was the guard he had tricked into the elevator only minutes ago.

"Jones! Get out here!" The guard was summoning the others.

Mark looked behind himself and saw the two federal agents rushing out of Herbie's apartment.

"Hold it, kid!"

Mark thought of the log book. If he waited, they'd take it away. They might even take him. He smiled at them for a moment and glanced in both directions again. The guards waited; they had no reason to suspect that he would not give up.

Mark nodded amicably to the guard in front of the elevator. The guard stepped forward, and as he did, Mark broke frantically into a dash down the open end of the hallway.

"Hey, kid! Come back here!"

Mark kept running. He heard the chime of the elevator door behind him. Then he heard Captain Munroe's voice. *"Don't come back 'til you have him!"*

The men were behind him, but Marie knew he had a chance. He knew Mega-20. They didn't. He had spent half his life hanging out here with Herbie. He knew he could escape. He kept running around the bend.

When the four federal agents rounded the corner, it was empty. "Fan out!" said Munroe. "I don't know what that kid wanted, what he heard or took, but we have to find out fast!"

The men spread out through the hallways, identifiers in hand. They banged at doors and checked stair cases, as they rapidly worked their way through each passageway. They circled through the apartment areas, coming at last down a rampway to some stores. They frantically checked each shop on the lower level. Munroe's nerves were about to snap when at last he spotted a figure running into a clothing shop.

It was the kid.

Cautiously, Munroe approached the store. Jones was behind him. Through a window, he spied the young man slipping toward the back. Casually, walking sideways, Munroe entered the store. He got within five yards before Mark saw him. Before Munroe could dodge them, two clothing racks tumbled to the floor. He was momentarily trapped.

"Come back here!"

Mark hurried toward the back of the store. He could hear the confusion behind him. Desperately, he positioned himself behind a stack of clothing crates. He could hear the agents, the sounds of store workers coming into the back, demanding to know what was happening. He leaned back, hoping they wouldn't spot him. Then he felt it. A metal casing. If he followed it, it would take him to a garbage chute. He'd have to risk being seen. Through a gap in the crates he spotted the agents flashing their badges to the people in the back of the store. "Government business," Munroe said. "I have to retrieve

something from that kid who went through here. Is there any way out of here?"

"Just the garbage chute," answered the manager.

Mark was already on his way.

The manager pointed, and as he did, Mark darted into sight. Munroe reached the gap in time to see Mark ducking into the chute. Realizing any further pleas or threats were useless, the captain ran to the chute. Munroe lifted his identifier for a shot. He aimed at Mark's vanishing body and fired.

Too late! The boy was gone.

They spent an hour checking the area on the other side of the chute, but Mark had disappeared. Munroe, his bald head shining with perspiration, reassembled his other agents and returned to Herbie's apartment. The Mega security forces outside had been told to disperse the crowds and open the travel-ways. Mega-20's sanitation people had disposed of the chips and scraps the explosion had littered about the lawn. It was beginning to look as if nothing had happened at all. The only things not returned to normal were the ugly scar on the outside of the building, and the interior of Herbie's apartment.

"All right, do we have everything together that we're going to get out of here?"

"Everything that kid left us, chief. The only thing we can remember that's missing is some sort of notebook."

"Don't remind me. I thought we'd lost him completely 'til Jones came up with that photo. I'm glad we put that identifier camera in Bender's bedroom."

"It's being processed now, sir," said Jones.

"Keep in touch with the lab. As soon as they have the print on that rebel, I want it. We have to find that kid, and find him fast. I think all of you know why."

The captain received no argument. "There's nothing more we can get done here," he said. "I don't know what he took. Let's pack it up and bus it on out."

Mark sat in a dimly lit cafe in Mega-8. He had hidden in different sections of Mega for a short time, trying to think of what he should do next. The longer he thought about it, the more he thought Herbie had been murdered. He had not seen a body, nor had he determined any reason for the murder, but he thought so just the same. He was so confused. He wanted to call his parents, but that too was a problem. How could he say, "Hi, dad, I'm on the run from federal agents?"

By now the identifier's findings had been processed, and he was known to Munroe's men through every public record with the name Mark Gutstein on it. They would have pictures of him, his fingerprints, his home address, a list of his friends—everything they would need to find him on a normal day. Which is exactly why he had run to Mega-8. He had never been there. Hardly anybody knew him in that part of town.

From the restaurant Mark had called his friend Mazzari. Despite their disagreements, he knew Mazzari could be trusted. He had to talk to somebody. He had to get some answers. He waited in the back of the restaurant, keeping to the shadows where it would be difficult to spot him, but where he could watch the front door. He was tense. He had broken security lines, run away from government officials. He had government evidence that belonged to Herbie. He clutched his jacket. The log book was secure.

Finally, after a twenty minute wait, Mazzari came through the door.

"Mazzari, man, what took you so long?"

"I'm sorry, Guts. I didn't want anybody to know what I was doin', what with your picture on the HV and all. I had to find you first."

"What do you mean?"

"Guts, I know you couldn't have done it!"

"Done what?"

"You didn't murder Herbie, did you?"

"Murder Herbie?! He was my best friend—why would I do that?"

"I don't know, Guts. The HV didn't say why, they just said that the government wanted you for questioning with regard to his murder."

Mark was stunned. "Mazzari, honest, you've got to believe me. The HV is talking loonie-flip. I wouldn't murder Herbie.

Are you crazy? I was home with my dad when the newsflash about the explosion came on HV!"

Mark told his friend everything. He explained what he had learned outside the building, how he had tricked the Special Forces men, of the things he had taken from the room, what he had seen inside, and of the chase.

"When I got to the bottom of the trash chute, I kicked my way free of all the crates and cardboard and hangers and ran. I ran to get away." Mark swallowed. He looked at Mazzari and said, "I'm scared, Mazz. I'm really scared. I think those agents murdered Herbie. I heard them talking with each other. Now they want me."

"The newsflash said you were suspected of tampering with sophisticated electronic equipment in Herbie's apartment. They said they found your fingerprints all over the room."

"Dammit, Mazzari, it's a lie!" Mark lowered his voice. Several people at other tables were looking. Mazzari pulled back in his seat away from Mark. "Listen, Mazz. I'm sorry I yelled, but I didn't do anything to Herbie. It's a trick! He had an old stereo in his apartment, not a bomb! I know the HV is lying. I didn't murder Herbie. I didn't. The federal agents must have told them that stuff. You have to believe me."

Mazzari was anxious to leave. "I believe you, but what are you goin' to do?"

"I don't know. I'd better get out of Mega for a while. Go somewhere else so I can think things out. Do you understand?"

Mazzari did not answer Mark. He sat silently, looking at his friend.

"Mazz, what's the matter? What is it?"

"You're going to *leave* Mega?" Mazzari said it as if he felt Mark was selling his grandmother into slavery.

"I have to leave. You think I'm pleased about it? They'll track me down in here. You know Mega. It's easy to find anybody. They'll find me too easy if I stay. There's no place I can really hide. I've got to get away."

"Guts, things'll work out! You got to trust the government. They know best—you know that."

Mark stopped talking. He had told Mazzari everything that had happened. Mazzari had to know he was innocent.

Mazzari touched his shoulder reassuringly. "Guts, I believe you. I mean, you're my pal. but you got to think clearly about this. There's got to be an answer, and I think the answer is to trust Mega."

"What do you mean?"

"Listen, the government would never want Herbie murdered, right? I mean, the jelly roll was a pain in the brain, but he would never hurt anybody."

"Of course," said Mark.

"Now, if we admit that it can't really be the government itself behind this, then it must just be that one batch of guys. The men that were there at Herbie's. Maybe they were crooks, or somethin', I don't know. Or just some Special Forces guys gone bad. We don't know, but we do know that nobody from Mega was involved. They were all federal guys, weren't they?"

"Yes, but . . . ."

Mazzari drew closer. He continued, "I'll call the security police. We'll tell them the story and give them the log book. They'll catch the guys that did this. The security police are from Mega. They may even know us. We can trust them."

Mark debated what his friend was saying. It made sense to him. It certainly made more sense than suspecting the entire government of some sort of plot to murder his best friend. That did not make any sense at all.

Mazzari smiled. "Think, Mark. If you keep runnin' from the Special Forces guys, they'll find you for sure. You can't beat the government. The government is on our side. They take care of us. They didn't do anything to Herbie. They'll just want to find out who did. You'll see. You have to trust the government, Guts."

Mark stared at his friend. "I'll tell you, Mazzari, I've been loonie since I first grabbed this book."

Mazzari nodded. He looked confidently at his nervous friend. "Let's call security and turn over this stuff."

Mark stood up. "Let's do it."

The pair had made their call to the police from the cafe, and they had been told to wait outside the front door. A Mega security man would come to pick up the book and explain everything to them. As they waited, Mark and Mazzari joked about "Guts, the Secret Agent" and "Guts's Big Adventure." It has all been a game. Mark had let his imagination get the best of him. No matter what things had happened in Herbie's apartment, the government couldn't really be responsible for murder. There was an explanation for everything, and as soon as the police had the book, they would find out what had really happened.

Still laughing, Mark spotted a government Special Forces man coming quickly down a walk near the cafe. There were five black and caramel uniformed men behind him, helmets in place, approaching them. Mark was silent. The man on the phone had said to expect one officer, and that he would be from the local police.

He whispered quickly to his friend, "Something's strange! Five guys, and they're wearing helmets, Mazzari! There's something happening and I don't like it! I'm running!"

"Guts, no, man! Wait! There's gotta be a reason!" Mark turned and ran. Mazzari stared at the approaching Special Forces men. Mark yelled, "Mazzari! Get out of there!"

Mazzari panicked. He knew the government would not harm him. He knew the government was good. He *knew* it, but when the Special Forces men aimed their lasers at him as well as Mark, he ran too.

Unfortunately, he had not started running soon enough. As Mark turned a corner, he peered back to see if Mazzari was going to make it.

A Special Forces man dove forward, one hand catching Mazzari's ankle. The young man made an effort to pull away, but another soldier caught up with him, smashing Mazzari into the wall. Mark cringed as Mazzari hit the concrete wall. There was no time to help him. He had to keep running. He had to get out of Mega!

As three of the Special Forces men continued after Mark, the remaining two held Mazzari. "This isn't the guy," said a gravel-voiced agent. "It's the guy in blue!"

The three agents chased Mark down a side walkway, up an abandoned path, and into Mega-5. After five minutes they realized they were lost. Mark had again used Mega to escape.

The troopers were respectfully silent. "Better get back to the other kid," said Jones, "maybe he knows where Gutstein is headed."

When they returned to the main walkway, a small crowd had gathered. Another federal agent, this time seated in a small electric car, had joined the other two and Mazzari.

"Colonel Donaldson," said Jones, "I have bad news."

"Don't tell me," said the colonel. Munroe looked angrily at Jones.

"The young man is more than we expected," said Donaldson. "Munroe, I want to see the records on this Gutstein at once!"

Mark sat shivering on an empty bench in the shadow of Mega-12. There was little alternative now. He knew he had to get out of Mega. They had murdered Herbie, and now they wanted him. It made no sense to him—he had never thought of Herbie as a wanted man. Yet there wasn't even time to figure it out. He patted his shirt to make sure the log book was still tucked inside and continued his winding route to the monorail station near Mega-2.

For an hour Mark had ducked passing squads of Mega security men and government troopers. He saw them in the shadows, in windows of normal apartments. As he ran, he thought he could be going mad, but he continued running west to the station. He had one objective—*Philadelphia*. The city was so large, so full of people, he'd be able to hide there. He knew little about it, but since the monorail was his only way out of Mega, he had little choice.

Mark headed into the gardens of Mega-2. He had had fewer close calls working his way through the parks of each building than in their halls and walkways. He knew he had to make the Metro before 1 a.m. The station closed at 1:05 every night. He looked at his watch. *12:35.* He was still a quarter of a mile away. He had been running and hiding most of the night. He needed sleep. He needed to talk to his parents. He needed to know that Mazzari was safe. There was no time.

Twenty minutes later, he was there. From fifty feet away, hidden by brush, he observed the monorail station entrance. He could see occasional blue and green uniforms on the platform.

The last train from Philadelphia had pulled into the station. It would be rerouted for the return trip in two minutes. In five minutes it would be gone.

He had to get on board. He saw federal agents in the station waiting. He'd have to get past them first. He thought about the monorail. Each of its cars was accessible from the one preceding or following it. There'd be a federal agent in every car waiting for him to get aboard. He could get on the train after it had been granted clearance to leave the station, but by then the doors would already be shut. There was no possible way for Mark to get inside the monorail before it left without being spotted.

Then suddenly he smiled. Who has to get inside? The troopers had all seen the pictures. They had all heard both the descriptions of Mark himself and the clothing he had worn in his escape from the apartment.

"Warren, anything at that end?"

"Nothing. Last of the Philly crowd is gone. A few commuters already are on the ride back to town."

"All clear at this end."

"Then let her slide." The security man waved to the engineer, giving him the word to pull the brakes. A pneumatic whoosh echoed in the station dome. The monorail began its slow build-up.

"I guess the kid's staying put."

"It looks that way. You'd better call Munroe!"

Mark was hidden several yards from the monorail. The cars took the slow incline to ground level and then made their way out of the dome. He ran for the monorail. He'd have thirty seconds before the car climbed the elevated track. He jumped for the space between the two cars. He had to grab one of the wide hooks beneath the coupling. He ran alongside the train, trying to get his other hand over the catch. He ran faster, stretching his hand. The train picked up more and more speed. The upgrade would increase sharply in seconds. His fingers slipped from the metal. Suddenly, there was no more ground beneath his feet. The train had begun its climb into the sky, its single rail gliding toward Pennsylvania. Luckily for Mark, the track curved as it went up. He had it! He pulled himself up by the hook. As the cars hugged a bump on the rail, Mark was slammed against the

35

coupling. He cut his jaw. He fumbled quickly, managing to wrap his arm around the coupling itself. The wind whipped at his dangling legs, and he felt the chill through his thin cotton pants. As the train picked up more speed, Mark pulled himself fully upward, finally reaching the small doorstep ledge on one of the two cars that faced him.

He kept his fingers tightly on the lip of the ledge, but it was little help against the jarring bumps of the monorail. Even if it had been, he had to grab the coupling and hang on every time the train lurched. At any moment, he could be thrown from the car. He leaned over the edge. He saw the New Jersey farmland fifty feet below him.

Mark huddled against the monorail door. He couldn't believe it. Yesterday he was watching a program on HV. Tonight he was hanging onto a train traveling at more than one hundred miles an hour through the night. He wanted to cry, but he didn't. He wouldn't permit himself to be frightened any more. He had to find out what had really happened to Herbie.

In fifteen minutes, if the monorail was on time, he would be in Philadelphia. He was determined to sit down and read the log book, and all the papers in it.

CHAPTER FOUR

As the monorail pulled into Philadelphia, Mark scanned the platform for security agents. Outside of a conductor walking up and down the platform, there seemed to be nobody of an official nature present. "Thank heaven for all little things. At least I wasn't spotted when I left Mega."

When the train came to a stop, Mark unwrapped his arms from the coupling and stood up. He ached. The circulation had stopped in both of his arms and one of his legs. He was sure of a cold and had odds on pneumonia. He jumped for the platform, but fell when he made contact. A few of the passengers looked at him but showed no particular concern.

The conductor helped him up. "Thought track-hopping had ended with the railroad," he said.

Summoning his strength, Mark stood up. He smiled at the conductor and headed toward a ramp with the other passengers. Mark had no real conception of Philadelphia, but here he was. He had escaped. He was free. He assumed that the city would be like Mega. Mark had been used to sameness. He came from a town where nothing was old, where hardly anything changed. He had seen thousands of pictures of cities on HV, but how different could a place only an hour from Mega be? Herbie had told him about Philly, but those were Herbie's stories. He often blew things up to seem more than they appeared.

At the bottom of the ramp Mark limped toward the station exit. He came out on Vine Street. It was 1:30 a.m. As he came out, however, he was stopped by the physical presence of the city before him. Slowly he looked around him. The sky was dark, but. . . . The plastic world of Mega which he had been expecting did not greet him. The buildings! Tall, short, dark, lighted! They were everywhere. Not all of the buildings connected. The streets were lined with cars. The walkways were hard, ungiving concrete like the walls of the buildings in Mega. He walked forward, looking at the buildings which surrounded the square outside of the Metrotram. Many of them were old—older than anything he had seen in Mega. He continued down the street, in fascination. There were signs everywhere—as if people needed them to know where to go. On each corner was a little sign. Block after block, he saw the words, "Vine Street." There was a small park nearby, and a few hundred yards in the distance he could see the enormous Ben Franklin bridge. He headed over to the park. It was deserted.

A few people passed him as he returned to Vine Street, young people in outlandish clothing, brilliantly colored costumes with hats and boots. Despite the late hour, the streets seemed alive. On a distant corner there was an open cafe. On another there sat a dingy tavern. Both open—at 1:30 a.m.!

In Mega, the streets and hallways of the city would be all but deserted.

Soon Mark found Vine Street growing even brighter. Various stores had lights on in their windows. A haze of neon-, fluorescent-, and moon-light threw shadows in all directions. There was a big corner ahead and on the top of a lampost Mark saw the words, "Broad Street." He knew he had to make a decision. Which way to turn?

Impulsively, he asked a passing stranger.

The man was old and shabbily dressed. "What you want, boy?" he said.

"I just wondered where I could find a hotel?"

"You want to flop out, boy?" The man looked at him anxiously.

"I need a place to spend the night. A hotel, or motel, or something."

"You fixin' to spend a bundle?"

Mark suddenly remembered he had left Mega with only a few dollars. "Ah, no, not actually. I only want to spend a little bit. I don't have much with me."

"Yeah, Monty knows. I got you. Listen. You take it on up Broad a ways. Ten, maybe twelve blocks. Maybe more. I ain't real sure. I do know the place is right on the corner. You won't miss it. Called the Holiday. It's not too bad a place. It don't cost a whole lot; I stayed there myself. Musta been twelve, thirteen years ago. For the Series!"

Mark smiled. "Yes, sir. Thank you." The people in Philly talked almost another language!

"It's on the left-hand side of the street," the man added. "You'll see it."

Mark thanked the man again and then started up Broad Street. He was impressed by the energy of the city even at that hour. There was a small row of stores filled with teenagers. The stores had pinball machines, a pizzeria, and an outdoor market selling magazines. There wasn't anything like it in Mega. The market was old, like it had been there for a hundred years. Although Mark was not sure why, "oldness" somehow seemed very important to him, very necessary.

Before Mark could take the thought any further, he found himself outside of the Holiday Hotel. He went inside to glance around the lobby. A skinny young man was sleeping behind the desk. Mark approached it and saw a small metal bell on the top. He rang it; the young man jumped up, straightened his cap, and said, "Twelve dollars, please."

"Twelve dollars?" asked Mark. "I don't *have* twelve dollars."

The young man sat down. "How much do you have, kid?" he asked.

Mark looked in his pockets. "Five-seventeen, but. . . ."

"I can give you a single bed," the young man said. "It's old but it's hard."

Mark frowned. "I need money for food. I don't think I can spend more than three dollars."

The young man smiled and rang the bell. "Sold!" he said, and he went to get a key.

Mark opened the door slowly, fumbling for the light switch inside. He clicked on an old glass bulb and looked around the room. There was an old bed, a dusty window, a broken chair, a wooden dresser, and a sign which said, "Check out time is 10 a.m. Thank you!"

Mark scratched his back. Not much, but he was anxious to use the shower. More than that, he was anxious to sleep. He had felt strangely safe in this city from the moment he had left the Metrotram station. He longed to call his parents, to tell them where he had gone, but he did not know if it was safe to call Mega. Mega—it seemed so very far away.

Mark sat down slowly on the edge of the bed. It was soft. He sighed and pulled the log book and papers from his shirt. He smoothed them out with one hand and placed the log book under his pillow. Then he walked across the room to shut off the light. As he did he looked back at the dusty window near the bed. "Hello, Philly," he said.

"Wake up."

Mark turned over in his bed. Something was disturbing him, but he tried to tune it out. There was a knocking and a voice again.

"Wake up time!"

The knocking grew more insistent, and Mark opened his eyes. Cautiously he asked, "Who is it?"

"Roomkeeper! Just here to clean out the room."

Mark opened the door. "I thought check out time was ten o'clock," he said.

"It's ten o'clock right now."

Mark looked embarrassed. "Oh wow, I'm sorry. Can you give me a few minutes?"

The old man looked at Mark. "Haven't seen you here. What's your name, kid?"

"Mark," he said cautiously. "Guts."

"Sure. You look as if you could use a bit more flop. Go back to bed. I'll start at the other end. They won't know the difference downstairs. You'll be set for a few more hours anyway."

"Well, if you think it'll be okay."

"Kid, you better get some rest. You look like you need the sleep. I'll wake you up later."

"Thanks, ah, Mr., ah. . . ."

"Cheeser. You just call me the Cheeser. That's what everybody calls me."

"Thanks, Cheeser."

"It's okay, Guts."

Mark smiled and shut the door as the old man went to the next door. As he returned to the bed, Mark knew he could not go back to sleep. He was worried. What if the old man recognized him? He seemed nice enough, but what if the HV in Philly had a newsflash like Mega's? Mark shook his head. He couldn't worry about *everybody*. He'd just wait and see.

He pulled the log book out from under his pillow and took out the papers inside. The first was a letter. It had been written to Herbie before he had finished high school.

Friend Bender:

Yes, you have indeed found the legend-gone-sour, the black sheep of Rock and Roll, the man who they all say was responsible for abandoning the music.

Yes, you have found me. I am yours. Do with me as you will.

Don't worry now. I don't want to sound too cynical right off the top. I appreciate your kind words about my music. It's nice to be remembered. I would never have thought that anyone in Mega under the age of forty knew what Rock and Roll was. Scratch that. What it *is*. I've been on the outside with the outsiders for so long, I'm beginning to think like them. That, my young friend, is a terrible thing.

So you are interested in Phil Spector's career. You would like to know what information I can tell you for your term paper. You came to the correct place. I can tell you about Spector all right. I knew him, as producer and friend for many years.

Phil was a madman and a genius. He drove his performers, hammering at them when they got lazy, molding bad notes into good, orchestrating beyond most musicians' fantasies.

If a bell tree, or a banjo, would improve a number, Phil would know it, would add it, and he would do it a hundred times to get it in place.

The letter continued onto a second page which Mark did not have. He picked another out of the pile. It was in the same handwriting.

Friend Herbie:

You write often, and you write much, but I tell you the same thing over and over again. David Star will not be coming out of retirement. I love your faith; it makes me fly. True. But, Herbie, you don't understand. There are whole volumes you don't know about me. Well, you don't know them yet, anyway. You will be coming to Philadelphia, save the questions until then.

I went over the music you wrote. You really wrote it? I mean, all of it, by yourself? If you did, it's very good. I would be forced to say excellent, actually. It really is great stuff, top liner and fine. And amazingly, it seems to be mainly written for guitar.

You're a tricky one, Herb. Maybe I will play it when you visit. But only for you. Not for a crowd. Fair enough? (But only if you rewrite those terrible words of yours.)

I wish I had more time, but I don't. I'll write more the next time. I promise.

Until later—keep after your work, and try to have some fun once in a while.

Hoping to see you,
David

They were only bits and pieces of letters, but slowly Mark began to pull the truth from them. The letters were all from a man named David Star. He and Herbie had written for some time while Herbie was still in high school. After Herbie had left for college, the letters had stopped.

From the tone of the letters, Mark found that he liked Star. The man seemed warm, receptive, as if he would have been a good friend for Herbie. Mark wondered why all of the letters were old, until it dawned on him that Star lived in Philadelphia. Once Herbie started school there, he didn't need to write. He and Star probably visited all the time.

Mark read all of the fragments. They were mostly about rock and roll, about Herbie's heroes from the past, musicians he had told Mark so much about when they were in high school together. There was something else, too. There was something he had wanted to tell Herbie. Something he wanted Herbie to know.

What could it be? Mark wondered. He had seen many detectives on HV; he had even read about a few in school. He felt like one of them, with pieces of a puzzle. He tried to make some sense of it all. *Whatever it was, I'll bet it is a clue to Herbie's strange behavior yesterday—clues to his disappearance.*

If only I had made him tell me what was bothering him, thought Mark. *I should have kept after him! He never talked about personal things. I should have pushed. . . .*

"Open up!"

There was a knock on the door. Mark held his breath. Agents? They couldn't have found him already! That old man—Cheeser. He called them. He had sold him out!

"Open up in there!"

Mark quickly gathered up the papers, stuffing them back into the log book. Grabbing up a lamp from the room's small dresser, he figured out a plan. He would wait until they opened the door, toss the lamp at them, and then run.

"Hey, Guts. Are you there, kid?"

"Yes, Cheeser! C'mon inside."

Mark reached for the lock. He would let the roomkeeper bring them in, and then he would move. As the knob turned, Mark lifted the lamp.

Cheeser came inside and Mark swiftly lowered the. . . .

"What are you doing with that thing?!"

Mark blushed. Cheeser was alone.

"What'sa matter with you, kid? You expecting trouble?"

"W—what makes you say something like that?" "Normal people don't swing lamps in the air. 'Cause you got hungry bar eyes, kid. The Cheeser has seen 'em all. Let me tell you. I know

45

you're runnin' from somethin'. Knew it since you went back to sleep."

"No." Mark was nervous. He wondered what the old man wanted.

"Don't worry. The Cheeser ain't goin' to bring the cops down on ya."

"Cops?"

"Old word. Sorry, I forget you kids don't talk the same as we did. The griefers, agents, the heavy handle, the police. You scan me?"

"Yes, but what's all that have to do with me?"

"Don't sweat it, kid. Listen. They want me just as bad as they do you, and they've wanted me longer. I don't know who you are, but I know what you are—you're a runner. Just like me. C'mon kid, tell me your side of the story."

Relieved, but still suspicious, Mark put the lamp back on the dresser. "I'm sorry about this—I thought—I was worried that. . . ."

"Hey, I know. It's cool. Tell me what's been goin' on in your life recently. Don't worry, I don't have anybody to tell. You're safe with the Cheeser."

Mark shook his head. "I'm not safe, Cheeser. I have to find David Star."

"David Star? The old rock musician? What's he got to do with you?"

"Nothing to do with me. He was an old friend of a friend of mine. I think maybe he'll let me stay with him. I have something of his to return."

"You a thief?"

"No!"

"I didn't think so. What do you want with an old rocker like Star? Are you one of those kids who runs away from home to become a big-shot musician?"

Mark looked out of the window nervously. This wasn't getting him anywhere. He knew he had to get moving fast, and he didn't like all the questions Cheeser was asking him. The roomkeeper could be stalling until the police arrived. *No,* he told himself, *you have to trust somebody here!* He looked at the old man. "Can you help me?" he said.

Cheeser nodded. "Guess so, long as it's something legal. Star's a legend. I haven't heard anything about him for a long time, but if he's in Philly I can find him. Philly's a great town for old rock and rollers."

"Why is that?" asked Mark.

"Used to be a lot of production around here. An old TV show called *American Bandstand,* an old studio called Sigma Sound, and a guy named Phil Spector. I'll tell you more about him later."

"That's going to help you find Star?"

"Yup. Guys like him all love to talk about their past."

"Why the past?"

"Kid, that's all they've got."

In exchange for his help in locating Star, Mark agreed to do the Cheeser's morning chores at the hotel. As he swept, scrubbed, and polished, the Cheeser made the rounds of old friends and bars.

Shortly after Mark finished the last room, the portly janitor returned with good news. He had a tip on Star. He also had a pile of clothing unlike any Mark had ever seen—heavy jeans, a rough blue plaid corduroy shirt, and an extremely bulky gray sweater.

"What is this stuff?" asked Mark.

"This is what you are going to wear out of here, Guts."

"Why?" As soon as he said it, Mark knew the answer. Camouflage.

Mark nodded. "Thank you, Cheeser."

While Mark changed into the new clothing, the old man told him what he had discovered. "Nobody has an address for Star, but here's a place where you might be able to find him on any night."

Cheeser handed him a piece of paper. "What is it?" Mark asked. He grunted as he did so. The jeans were a bit tight.

"It's an old bar in South Philly called the Piper. It's sort of a meeting place for old rock and roll lovers. They go there to hear their favorite old tunes. Sometimes a leftover from the '50's or early '60's will get up there and croak out a tune and everybody flips. Word is that David Star has been seen in there."

"Terrific!"

The Cheeser grew quiet. "Guts," he said.

"Yeah?"

"Listen, I've done some other digging, too. You know zero about cities. Mega ain't really a city, it's some sort of shopping mall gone wild."

Mark couldn't hide his surprise. "Mega? What makes you think I'm from Mega?"

"Word travels fast even from the sticks. Don't worry, I know you ain't no killer. I know you're straight. Man, are you straight. Philly's not Mega. You're going to have to be careful, Mark. I mean, Guts. You're lucky you don't have anything to steal."

Mark eyed the log book on the bed.

"What's that?" said the Cheeser.

"Something to steal," Mark said uneasily.

Cheeser frowned. "Hide it. I mean it. If you're on the run, you're going to attract trouble like fly paper."

Mark nodded. "Where can I hide it?"

"Someplace busy," said Cheeser. "Someplace easily accessible."

"Like a monorail station?"

The Cheeser smiled. "You've been watching old movies, kid. That's a good idea. The train station is a good idea."

Mark nodded. He had the sweater and shirt on now. They were big, much too big. "I think I should buy just the pants, Cheeser."

Cheeser laughed. "Buy 'em? They're a gift, kid! Nobody else would put 'em on anyhow."

"They are tight."

"They don't shout 'Mega', kid. Wear 'em. I'm sorry about the sweater."

Mark smiled. "It's nice of you to get me the clothes at all. I gotta tell you, I don't know what I would have done without you."

"You got a lot of heart, Guts. It'll take you a long way. You're in the city now. You've got to learn to use your smarts. You're afraid of something big. I can tell. Now all I want to say to you is, there's no reason to be scared. You remember that, Guts. Whatever they've run on you, you just remember who you are.

Don't run away from anything, don't be afraid of it. Just think things through before they get to you. Okay?"

"Okay." Mark grinned.

"We better get goin' if we're goin' to get you a locker. I think we can get a SEPTA tram from the monorail station."

Mark opened the door.

As the Cheeser turned out the lights, Mark placed the log book back inside his shirt. He fell in line behind the old man as they headed down the hall.

"Cheeser," said Mark as they reached the stairs to the lobby, "why are ya doing this for me?"

Cheeser shook his head. "Don't ask."

"Why?"

"Kid, one of the saddest things in the world is not having a second chance! Look at me. I'm a janitor. Nobody helped me when I was young. They said, 'Get a job.' I got it. I have it. Did you ever think about spending your whole life in one place day after day after day?"

Mark thought about Mega.

"It's like being in prison, kid. I've been there, too. I'll do anything legit to keep another kid out. You're entitled to a life, Guts, not just an existence."

CHAPTER FIVE

Mark and the Cheeser were outside the Metrotram station. They had hidden the log book in a locker, and were on their way to meet David Star when Mark asked the Cheeser to wait.

"There's something I have to do," he said quietly. "Something I've been thinking about ever since I left Mega."

"You want to call your parents, right?"

Mark was surprised. "How did you guess?"

"It don't take much. You eyed that communication room over there and every other phone since we left the hotel. It was easy to figure out what ya wanted to do."

Mark started for the phone. "It'll just take me a minute. I'll be right back."

"You better not take any more than that."

"Huh, why not?"

"You're hot, kid. They probably have a trace on your home phone already. You talk more than a minute or two, and they're goin' to know where you are, right down to the exact phone."

Mark thought for a second. At present, the Special Forces did not seem to know he was in Philadelphia. He knew the Cheeser was correct. He had seen enough HV to know about the phone traces, but he also knew his parents. They would be crazy with worry. As far as they knew, he was a fugitive from justice. No matter what, Mark had to reach them. Mark walked over to the pubphone, dropped in **a** coin, and punched a set of numbers. The phone buzzed once and he heard his father's voice.

"Hello?" His father sounded nervous.

"It's me, dad!"

"Mark! Thank God. Are you all right? Where are you—don't answer that! Don't tell me where, Mark, but tell me what's happened!"

In the background Mark could hear his mother. "Mark? Is it Mark?"

He knew there was only a minute to talk. His father told him not to say where he was. Then his dad also knew the phone was being bugged! "Dad, I'm safe. I just wanted to tell you I'm safe. I have somebody helping me."

"Get a lawyer, son, get a lawyer," his father said.

Then his mother got on the phone. "Darling, we're trying to find out what happened. We know you're innocent. We're waiting for word from the local police."

Mark shook his head. "No," he answered, "not the police, the federal agents have control over them, too!"

His father got back on the line. "Don't worry, Mark. We'll clear it up for you. Just stay safe! I...."

There was a click on the phoneline.

"Hang up, son!" Mark's father said quickly.

Mark obeyed.

There was a silence. He turned and faced Cheeser. "We'd better start out," said the roomkeeper. "There may be agents here any moment!"

Mark nodded. He wished he could call his parents back, but he knew Cheeser understood the game better than he did. He wished he could make some sense of it all.

Mark and Cheeser waited across the street from an old bar in South Philadelphia. Although he wanted to go inside, he was hesitant. This part of the city was something Mark had never experienced. The people were dressed in old, dark clothing. They were sullen and unsmiling. There was nothing cheerful about most of the streets the Cheeser had taken him down.

"This ain't Mega, Guts. There's only poor people livin' around here. You've never been out of the Mega complex before, have you?"

"My family went to Chester once."

"Another hamburger town!"

"Hamburger town?"

"Yeah. That's what poor folk call the new towns. The government grinds them out and tells us they're terrific."

"Just like hamburgers?"

"Exactly. Mega's no place for me. I couldn't get a job there. There ain't nothing for old men in one of those places. Oh, I know, they'd put me on federal aid—yeah sure, but that's not what I want. I want to work. I like to work."

Mark said nothing further. He followed the Cheeser through the broken back streets of the city.

"There's a lot to be done," said Cheeser. "There's always a lot to be done, but I'll take Philly over Mega any day. At least here I have some sense of place! Philly's got a past, Guts! A sense of history. People have lived here Mark. All sorts of things have happened, some good, some bad, but all of them real."

Mark looked at the streets around him. Some were darkened alleyways, others had broken bottles in the streets. Yet there were also beautiful old brownstone buildings within sight and shiny new structures in the skyline only blocks away.

Five minutes later, Cheeser rested against a lampost on a sidestreet. "Guess you're on your own now, Guts. You're going to have to find out things for yourself."

Mark looked at the Cheeser. He was nodding toward a dusty neon sign across the street. It was flashing "The Piper," only the first "P" was missing. It looked funny.

"That's it!" said Mark. "I just don't know how to thank you, Cheeser. For the money, the hotel, even the jeans."

"Don't thank me for the jeans, kid! As for the help, you just get yourself clear of whatever they tagged on you. That's enough thanks for me."

"You have my word, Cheeser."

"Good luck, kid!" The roomkeeper smiled, and the two men shook hands, knowing they would probably never see each other again. Then the Cheeser disappeared through an alley across the street. Mark stood outside the Piper for a long time. He had never been in a bar, and he was worried. "What if somebody wants to see my ID? I'm not old enough to get in there yet, but if I don't show my ID, they may call the police.

If I do show it, they'll see my name, and by now, they probably know it from HV."

Pennsylvania's drinking age was still twenty-one. Mark was not sure just how much age the darkness would lend him. He knew, however, that he had to find David Star, and he knew the only place to look was the Piper. Mark looked at his watch, it was 10 p.m. If he's coming down for a drink tonight, he thought, then he's probably there by now.

Mark started down the stairs to the Piper. It wasn't crowded inside, but the heavy smoke and noisy back room made it seem like it was. The music sounded familiar, like something Herbie had once played for him. As Mark walked toward the bar he looked around the room. Those who had watched his entrance had already returned to their drinks. The place was filled with antiques from thirty years ago. Hanging planters were tied to the ceiling. A strobe light flashed in a corner of the room. There was a juke box on the wall near the bar. It was playing a song called "Love Me Tender." For long seconds Mark peered through the smoke trying to spot Star. "This is crazy," he said to himself. "I don't even know what he looks like."

Mark walked to the bar. He thought of something the Cheeser had told him. "Philly's got its nice places and its tough places. If you come up against some cruncher who could take your head off and hand it to you, out-think him, out-guess him." Mark realized he'd have to be thinking *very* fast to get any information about Herbie or David Star.

He approached the bartender, an older man with a heavy beard and handsome features that had not been diminished by the years.

"What will you have?" the bartender said.

Mark tensed up. "I'll have some information," he said bravely.

"Information?"

"I'm looking for a man called David Star."

"Who wants to know?" asked the bartender cautiously.

"I do."

"Why?"

"I have something of his. Something that belonged to a friend. I think he might be interested."

The bartender was starting to get him nervous.

"You don't come into a place like this and ask for a man that way," he said softly. "Who are you?"

"Guts," said Mark in a deep voice. "Just call me Guts."

Then the bartender smiled. "You're a tough character."

Mark blushed. The bartender was onto his act already. He should have known better than to fake it.

"Don't take it too hard, Guts," said the bartender. "You're new at the game."

"Huh?"

The bartender extended his hand. "I'm David Star."

Mark beamed. "You are?"

The bartender nodded. "Now listen," he said. "Herbie told me about you many times. I don't know how you got involved in this mess, but I know they're after you. You're in serious trouble, Mark."

Mark nodded. "I don't know much. I was hoping you could tell me something. I'm scared."

Star stared at him. "I can't tell you anything."

"Nothing? Nothing about why Herbie was attacked?"

Star shook his head. "Too dangerous."

"I have Herbie's log book," Mark explained.

Star drew back. "For God's sake, you don't have it here, do you?"

"No."

Star looked relieved. "You've hidden it?"

"In a safe place."

Star's agitation subsided. He was about to speak when somebody down the bar called for service. "Please stay here," he whispered.

Star took care of the customer and then returned to Mark. Coming closer, he whispered, "Get the log book, but don't bring it here." Reaching down behind the bar, Star tapped out an address on a tiny computer terminal. He tore off the paper readout and handed it to Mark.

As the young man took it, he noticed that Star's fingers were covered with small cuts. There was no time to comment on them, though. Star wanted him to get the log book. "Meet me at this address," said Star.

Mark nodded nervously. "When?"

"Tonight. Two o'clock."

"In the morning?"

"That's the only two o'clock tonight I know."

"Why so late?"

"I don't get off until one. I just can't leave. It'll cause suspicion."

Mark smiled. "I'll be there."

Star was not smiling. "Be careful," he said. "I've been through this too many times. They're playing for high stakes, Mark. I'm sorry you're involved. There's no turning back, though. I need you. I know you have a thousand questions, but they'll just have to wait. The government knows they can't touch me. I'll explain later. Now we have to worry about them catching you. I want you to leave through the back. Sit down there first. It'll look less suspicious."

Mark headed back to a cafe behind the bar.

There was a band on stage in the back. Mark sat down and listened as they started to play.

It was the first time he had ever heard live rock and roll music. He had never met anyone except Herbie who had. He was confused. He had always heard that viddiscs were the greatest musical experience there could be. "Computer-coded for quality sound." He had always been told that was the reason why synthenization was rarely performed like this music was. It was more complex, more "sophisticated." Yet this music was something else. He sat there listening, longer than he should have, to number after number. Surprisingly, although he could not really figure out why, he was thrilled. There was something in the music, something vital. Viddiscs could not compare. What was it? How could music like this have been allowed to disappear? The steady droning beat of synthenization was gone. It had been replaced by an irresistible energy, a rhythm and harmony which pulsed and shouted. Before Mark realized it, he was clapping in time with the rest of the customers. He unconsciously tapped his foot to the beat.

He had always known there was a certain bounce to Herbie's music, but the old scratching discs he played on his antiquated stereo had not shown Mark a glimmer of what he was now feeling about the band and its music.

The band's guitarist spoke to the audience for a moment to explain the nature of their music. As he talked, Mark knew it was time to leave. It was 12:30. He had to get back to the Metrotram station and the log book. Then he had to discover a way to get to the address on the printout. He slipped out the back door of the bar inconspicuously.

He wasn't looking forward to the trip, but he knew that an answer to the mystery was within reach. He'd make it, he had to make it!

He had made it safely back to the Metrotram station. Unlike the main station, it was rather deserted. Once inside, he headed for the lockers. Fishing into his pocket, Mark pulled the key out and checked the number. He put it in the slot and pulled out the log book. He shoved it into his shirt, closed the locker, and hurried back toward the station doors. Then he heard the sound of footsteps. Although there did not seem to be anyone behind him, Mark was convinced he had heard them.

He jogged faster toward the doors, but after another few steps, he heard the noise behind him again. Somebody was following him. More than one person, two, maybe three.

It can't be Special Forces, he thought. *They wouldn't bother to sneak up. They'd just grab me.*

As Mark reached the edge of another long row of lockers, he glanced back. There were three of them, of indeterminate age in the darkness, all dressed for action. Undistinguished clothes. Easy to hide. Hard to identify. Muggers. Cheeser had cautioned him.

Mark started running. They were closing in on him, shouting funny names at him, trying to frighten him.

"Hey, good-looking!"

"Hey, are you an athelete?"

"Hey! What's the hurry!"

He saw a sign to the SEPTA subway system. If he could get there, if he could get to the entrance, maybe there'd be a guard or a teller or. . . .

"Hey, handsome!"

The footsteps went silent behind him. Mark turned for a second in surprise and saw a small, blue glass sphere whizzing toward him. A flarephasing! Before he could close his eyes, the ball hit a wall and broke open. There was a flash of light, temporarily blinding him. Mark shouted for help, but there were three shadows around him. His eyes started to clear, but it was too late. The three shadows were pulling at him, tearing at his shirt.

"Help!" Mark shouted again.

The muggers kept pulling at him. Tugging at his clothes. Suddenly there were the sounds of other footsteps in the hall.

"Clamp it and pace!" yelled one of the gang. "It's the police!"

Mark stumbled for a second as the muggers took off. He was dizzy, he was still having a hard time seeing, but at least....

"You! Don't move!"

The haze lifted and Mark saw the men who had rescued him.

There were two government agents coming down the hall.

"It's him!" yelled the first. "It's the kid from Mega!"

"Don't move, kid!" said the other agent, but Mark had learned his lesson in Mega-20. These guys were crazy. He wasn't waiting for anybody!

Before he could catch his breath, Mark headed in the direction of the subway. Minutes later he grabbed the railing at the top of the subway stairs. He jumped on top and pulled an old trick from Mega. Sliding down the railing, he hit the platform at the bottom of the stairs feet first.

The local train was clunking into the station.

"Open up," Mark screamed, "it's gotta open up!"

He heard the sound of the agents' footsteps on the stairs behind him.

The doors of the local slid open, and Mark ran inside the first car. He wasn't safe. He knew it. They'd be inside and find him before they got to the next station. He looked around the subway car. It was empty. No place to hide. He was trapped.

"Next car!" came a voice outside.

They were onto him. He had to get out! The doors started to close. Mark rushed to the front of the car. The guards were at the back. He looked at the front of the car. The tracks were starting to disappear underneath the car. The subway was moving.

He looked behind him. The men were closing in fast. Ten seconds and he'd be trapped. The agents had no weapons. They were obviously supposed to bring him back.

He felt the log book slipping down his shirt toward his pants. He could not let them have it now. Not after what happened to Herbie. Not after his commitment to Star. To Cheeser. To himself! He had to know what happened to his best friend before he faced the government.

He had to escape!

He whirled away from them, and pulled the emergency brake on the ceiling of the car. The train lurched suddenly backwards. The agents toppled, as if a rug had been pulled out from under their feet.

Mark spun around again, and darted between them. A bell was ringing now. The train was on automatic. It could go nowhere until reset. He knew it from riding the monorail around Mega. He also knew how to get out.

As the agents recovered, Mark kicked the door at the back of the car. It did not move.

He kicked it again, hitting his boot against the hard lucite window.

It did not move.

He kicked *the window* again and...

...it popped out!

Safety precaution. Like on a bus. Mark jumped through, scraping his arm as he did.

The agents were behind him. But he was free.

In the darkness.

He was scared again. He was in between stations, in a subway tunnel he did not know. "Gotta hold on, now," he told himself. "There's got to be a station ahead of me."

Then he remembered what Cheeser had told him. *Think fast.*

He spotted the agents coming out from the car into the tunnel. He thought fast. He ducked under a coupling between the next two cars and vanished.

If they were thinking about the next station as he had, then he would head back to the station they'd just left!

CHAPTER SIX

It was morning. Mark was in the vacant lot at the address Star had given him the previous evening. He had arrived at 2:30. Now the sun was up. Star had never shown.

"Dumb!" Mark said to himself. "I had to get in trouble! I must've missed him." He had fallen asleep at 3:30. The sunlight woke him. A scab had congealed on his arm. There were rocks cutting into it. Slowly, stiffly, he stood up. He took a few steps, walking around to examine the area in daylight.

They must be getting ready to build something here, he thought. This place is a disaster area! He remembered his escape last night, back to the deserted station, past the Metrotram station to the street. He had run like a madman, up streets, down alleys, in the most confusing pattern he could make. At last, with help from a man at a gas station, he had found the lot. Now he was worried. The agents had had all night to find him. Philly *was* bigger than Mega, but they had more men in the city.

"Mark?"

Gutstein turned. There was a girl, coming through the brick archway of a former brownstone building.

"Mark Gutstein?"

He hid behind a brick wall. Who was she?

"Mark?"

Then he heard a laserblast.

It seared through the edge of the archway and the girl dove for cover.

"Mark! Answer me!" she shouted, and then she started running toward the center of the wreckage. That was insane thought Mark, she'll be a moving target! Mark looked behind him and saw a Federal Special Forces officer on a rooftop with a laser. Whoever the girl was, she had to be more of a friend than the agent. Or was she a decoy to get him off guard?

Mark didn't know.

That feeling of paranoia was setting in again, of not knowing, how—what....

Another laserblast! Mark knew there was no time for questions.

"Here!" he yelled. He had to trust somebody. "Over here!"

The girl ran toward him, but as she did another laserblast hit the brick.

"Keep to the ground!" Mark yelled. He was getting to be an expert on escape.

"Mark! Thank God! I thought we'd lost you to the government!"

She hid with him behind the wall. Thin, brown hair, assertive. About twenty-two years old.

"Come on," she said, "no time to lose!"

"Who are you?" Mark asked firmly. "I have to know before I run any further."

"Are you bananas? He's shooting at us. Run!"

Mark dashed for the street hand-in-hand with the girl.

Another shot clipped past them. Laser fire sizzled the trail, blasting chips of stone in the ruins around them. As Mark tried to turn one way, the girl grabbed his arm again and pulled him to the left. "This way."

"You sure?"

"You want to argue?"

Mark followed her. They twisted around a corner and finally escaped the range of the rooftop sharpshooter who had been firing at them. Mark started to slow down, but the girl tugged at him. "Keep going. They have the area surrounded."

"Where are we going?"

"To my apartment." The girl smiled. "I know you're scared. Just keep moving. We'll make it."

"Who are you?" Mark asked again.

"Not now," said the girl. "Not until we get there." They jogged forward, twisting through the ruined buildings. Voices rang out around them. Several times they were forced to stop and hide as they dodged another Special Forces attack. The girl seemed to know where she was going.

Mark ran, dodging another shaft of red which tore through a storefront next to them. The girl pulled him toward a long alley. "This way!" she said. They ran down it. As they ran, Mark cried, "What are you doing, girl? There's no street on the other side!"

"Keep going, Mark." And as he did, he heard a pair of agents turn into the alley behind him. "Over here. We got them cornered now."

"Hurry," yelled the girl.

"Where?"

They were at the end of the alley. Ahead was a pile of rotten wood and mud. To the left and right were brick walls and an old sidewalk.

"In the street, lunkhead! In the street!"

Mark stared at the pavement. There was a four-foot-wide metal circle in the middle. He had seen them all over Philly. They didn't have them in Mega. "What is it?" he said.

The girl frowned. "I don't believe it!"

"Do not move!" came a voice at the other end of the alley. "We have you surrounded."

"Idiot!" The girl pushed Mark out of the way and grabbed one of the holes in the center of the circle. "It's a manhole cover," she said. She pulled it up and handed it to Mark.

Red-faced and sweating, he stared back at her.

"Throw it!" she said angrily. "Throw it at them!"

She ducked into the manhole. He faced the oncoming agents. There was the sound of a laser, and a second later the manhole cover caught a blazing red flare.

"Drop it!" shouted the girl. "Jump inside! Come on, Mark! Get down here!"

Mark jumped into the manhole and landed in a bed of thick brown mud.

"Yecchh!"

The girl was waiting. "Come on Mark. We have a long way to go."

They started down the sewer tunnel, wading through two feet of mud and water as they walked.

The tunnel branched off twice, feeding into other streets. The girl proceeded without hesistation. Far off in the distance, they could hear the echoes of the agents searching the tunnels. After thirty minutes, however, the sounds had disappeared.

"You know exactly where you're going, don't you?"

"Exactly," said the girl.

Mark rested against the tunnel wall for a minute. The smell was terrible. His clothes were covered with mud and slime. As they had waded quickly through the sewer system, an occasional ripple could be seen in the water. Rats.

Yet the girl went on, unflinching. She had hardly said a word to him, except to direct him through the tunnel.

"I gotta rest," said Mark.

"When we get to my apartment." She pulled him.

"Who are you?" Mark asked. "I've trusted you this far. You have to tell me."

The girl nodded solemnly. "I thought you'd have known by now. I'm David Star's daughter."

Munroe sat in the front seat of a silver jeep. In the back were three federal agents, all covered with mud.

"That kid! I thought the kids were supposed to be docile now!" He talked angrily to the empty seat next to him. "They were supposed to be under control! They were supposed to be content! So what do I get? A Mega rebel and a mystery woman!"

A light on his console flashed.

"Message for you," said one of the agents from the back seat.

Munroe picked up a phone from the jeep's console. "Yeah?" he said, "Munroe speaking."

The voice on the other end was loud and anxious. "You got him, Munroe? You got him this time?"

It was Colonel Donaldson.

"There's a slight problem," said Munroe gently.

"Problem! What sort of problem!" The colonel was furious. "*Munroe?* Are you there?"

Munroe placed the receiver on the empty seat of the jeep. "I'm having trouble hearing you," he shouted.

"Munroe? Munroe?" After two minutes of shouting, the colonel hung up.

The captain put the jeep into first gear. As he pulled out of the abandoned four block area in South Philly, he shook his head. "This has been nothing but trouble from the start. We have it coming to us, too. I told Donaldson, I told the government, they should never have gotten into it!"

The jeep rolled slowly ahead. Sunlight bounced playfully off Munroe's bald head. In a way, he was glad the attack force had failed. The kid didn't deserve what they had waiting for him. He knew there'd be heat from Donaldson at headquarters. The chase was still on and he was to blame. He'd do as he was ordered, but it was a stupid mission. Stupid from the start.

David Star's daughter and Mark rushed through a darkened alley, their clothes covered with mud and garbage. Each looked like some sort of bizarre scarecrow, filled with slime instead of straw.

"Hurry up!"

Both were relieved. They had exited through a sewer near the girl's apartment, unsure of whether there would be government agents waiting for them.

The alley was empty.

"Come this way!" the girl whispered. They slipped through the door of a stately apartment building.

Twenty minutes later, they huddled in the bathroom of a small apartment. The girl called it a "studio." It was unlike any apartment Mark had seen. It was old, the floors were wood, and there were high ceilings crisscrossed by rectangular bars. Mark liked it.

"Nice, uh. . . ."

He still didn't know the girl's name.

"My name's Jessica. Sorry for the secrecy, Mark."

Mark smiled. "It's all right. You saved my life. I can understand why you had to keep quiet."

He had been running so long that it was starting to seem as if danger was normal.

Jessica looked at him angrily for a second.

"Did I say something?" Mark asked.

"No." Jessica turned away from him and pulled off her sweater.

"I'll shower first," she said. "Here's a towel, at least you can wipe off your face."

Mark didn't know what to say. He took the towel and started to sponge his cheeks. The bathroom door closed behind him.

* * *

Jessica had changed into a fresh shirt and pants, much like the set she had been wearing earlier. Mark soaked his clothes while taking a shower. A special heater under Jessica's sink had made them dry enough to wear.

"I guess your dad's gonna meet us here," said Mark. "I'm sorry I missed him last night. I had trouble."

Jessica looked grim. "My dad never made it to the lot," she said. "He's missing. I think they got him last night, Mark. I think the government took my father."

Mark was shocked. "It can't be! He sounded so calm when I saw him. He knew what was happening! He told me they couldn't touch him."

Jessica sighed. "He's been at it so long that he never shows how he feels. The government's getting nervous. I'm scared, Mark. My father told me what you have. I was supposed to go with him last night. That little trip through the sewer was planned for the three of us. Now dad's vanished—like Herbie. I know why he wanted to meet you."

"I have the log book, Jessica." Mark tried to look comforting. "That's what your father wanted from me. I'll get it now." He went into the bathroom and brought it out. It was muddied, but the papers and record were intact.

Jessica looked at it anxiously. "It must be in here, Mark. It must have the clue! Dad told me it did! We have to solve the puzzle, Mark. We have to do it now."

"Hold on," Mark said. "What *puzzle?* What clue? You mean you *know* what's important in here? It's been driving me crazy since I took it!"

Mark told Jessica his entire story. She knew a little bit already. She knew all about Herbie and the log book. She knew all about her father. David Star had confided in her, told her, almost

71

everything, leaving out special bits of information to protect her. Mark told her the circumstances behind the explosion. He told her that he was quite sure that Herbie had been murdered. When he had finished, he looked at Jessica. She seemed angry.

"You're not helping me," she replied at first, "if Herbie's been murdered then. . . ."

"I'm sorry," said Mark.

Jessica walked away from him. "It's all right. It's not your fault. I know the Special Forces. I have to think about it, too. My dad could have been murdered. Chances are more likely that dad got it than Herbie."

"Don't talk like that, Jessica!"

"Shut up!" She walked over to the window. She was crying.

Mark slowly approached her. "Jessica," he felt a choking in his throat, "what's going on here? I'm scared. I've never really been out of Mega before, or even lived away from my mom and dad! I've been running for two days now, Jessica! I just want to go home and find my friend safe!"

He was crying now, too. He hugged Jessica. She comforted him.

"Jessica, what is it? Why are they after us? What's the puzzle? What does the log book have to do with the government? What would federal agents want with *anybody* from Mega?"

Jessica faced him. "Mark, Mega is a test center. The people in it are slowly being controlled."

"Controlled? Are you kidding? How?"

"Through electronic communications, mostly. The HV, viddiscs, radio. . . ."

"The HV?" Mark pondered that for a moment. It seemed strange. "How could HV or viddiscs do anything to control the people in Mega?"

"Mega and the other new towns in the East are prototypes," said Jessica. "They're using them to test what the government secretly calls behavioral control systems. *BCS*."

"*BCS?* It sounds like a skin cream."

"You wish. It's a secret program, Mark, but if it works in Mega, they're going to try to use it on the entire country. What's worse, they'll think it's *good* for us, too."

"What *is* it, Jessica?"

"It's a coding system, Mark. It's meant to change the way we act. I *mean* us—not old people, not babies—*us*. Young people. People who are still forming their ideas about life."

"C'mon, Jessica, no HV program or viddisc is going to teach me what to do!"

"Oh no? It already has!"

Mark stared out the window. Was this all a trick? To make sure he wasn't a government spy? No, Jessica was serious. He knew it.

"They've got a message built into everything, Mark. Especially synthenization."

Mark shook his head. "Synthenization may not be very good music, Jessica, but it's not brain washing me. It's not making me do something I don't want to do."

Jessica smiled. "That's true. It's not making you do anything. It's making you *not* do anything! Like a sedative. That's part of what my father discovered. There's a message in synthenization music, and my father knows what it is. That's one reason why the government has been after him."

"Wait a minute. The government doesn't make synthenization."

"No, it doesn't, Mark, but it knows the people that do."

"Huh?"

"The federal government is a big machine, Mark. Some of it works *to our advantage*—like the part that sends money to old people when they're too sick to pay for doctors. There's another part that works with big companies—record companies, manufacturing companies, clothing companies. That's called the FTC."

Mark nodded. "*The Federal Trade Commission.* We learned about it in school."

"Good, then you understand me. You see, when the government is working smoothly, one part of it helps another, but today some of the parts of government are working *too* close. Like the Environmental Renaissance Agency and the FTC."

"I still don't understand, Jessica. What does the FTC have to do with Mega?"

"Who designed Mega, Mark?"

"I don't know! The government, I guess."

"Not exactly. The government hired private corporations to design it. Those private corporations were selected by the Environmental Renaissance Agency."

"So what?"

"So once Mega was finished, those same corporations still wanted to make money from Mega! To do that, they made sure to design it in a way that only they could service."

"By putting in things only they knew how to work?"

"Bingo!"

"That's not bad, is it?"

"It is if you like to have a choice."

"I like Mega the way it is."

"Yeah, but *why* do you like it? Why is it better than any other town?"

"I don't know about any other town."

Jessica smiled. "You're getting the picture."

Mark nodded. He didn't know what she was talking about yet, but it was getting clearer.

"Let's say companies, like McDonald's, or even the people that make viddiscs, were responsible for designing Mega. As a result, they have their stores in Mega already and are doing a lot of business. In business you're only as good as what you sell. What if you can't sell any more than you're already selling? The people who run your company get worried. They aren't making any more money."

"What if they were making the *same* amount of money, but no less?" asked Mark.

"They wouldn't be very happy about it. They'd get worried. They'd look for ways to make people buy more of what they're making. Maybe they'd use a silly song—they're called jingles. Or maybe they put a commercial on HV. *Then what happens?* What if they've made *all* the commercials and sung *all* the jingles? *What* then? What if everybody who wants hamburgers and viddiscs have them?"

"Well, they can't make other people buy what they don't want."

"That's true, Mark. So they have to make the other people *want* first. Crazy, huh?"

"You mean they use something like mind control? We studied that in Mega. It's illegal. It's against the Constitution. If a company did that, they'd lock it up!"

"That's where *BCS* comes in, Mark. That's where the federal government machines come in again, too. Certain companies have come up with a way to influence people's minds in what they call a 'good' way. They say it's not for *products* but for *health* and *social welfare.* They've gotten permission from their friends at the FTC to test it. Test it right in the new towns like Mega."

"I think that's a little far out, Jessica."

"Oh, do you? How many people smoke in Mega?"

"None. It's illegal. Everybody knows that tobacco is a poison. It's on HV."

"Yeah, but people poison themselves with tobacco every day in Philly. I don't like it, but isn't it funny that nobody at all does it in Mega? Not even behind the back of the government officials?"

"Are you saying the BCS makes people not smoke?"

"That's just an example, Mark. The companies have convinced the FTC that they have a way to *electronically* eliminate undesirable actions in the public sector."

"*Public sector?*"

"You. Me. Kids. They say they can make us 'better' people by putting BCS in HV, viddiscs, even radio."

Mark shook his head. "How do they do it?"

"It's complicated to explain. I'll give you an example. Think of how they make a movie for HV. You know how they're made?"

"Sure. There are lots of little pictures, one after another. Each picture slightly different than the picture before it. When they run together, it makes a moving picture."

"You got it, Mark. Suppose you added an *extra* little picture, right in the middle of the others. Just a little picture with a message on it. Do you know what would happen?"

"Nobody'd see it. It would be on and off the screen too quickly."

"Nobody'd *think* they saw it, but they *would* have. They'd remember it, too. That's called *sublimination.* That was just the start of BCS. BCS is a thousand times more sophisticated—and it is most sophisticated in the music."

"Why is that?" asked Mark.

"Music is possibly the fastest way to use BCS. You can feel the bass. You can hear the sound. You *think* about the music. That's why synthenization was invented. It's computerized music, it's easy to manipulate, easy to plant messages into it. The companies have found a way to program synthenization with certain messages. The kids in Mega listen to synthenization all the time, so they get the same messages all the time. It's been programmed through computer. It's encoded on the viddiscs and it's sent out when you play the viddiscs at home. They're making *puppets* of kids, not people. The messages they're giving them are simple. 'Buy this!' 'Don't do that!' It's all in the interest of the companies and the government."

Mark was angry. "I'm not a puppet! I'm here, aren't I?"

Jessica smiled. "Are you? Yes, but did you ever do anything else out of the ordinary in Mega before Herbie disappeared? Did you ever want to travel? To see things you never saw? Or were you always happy doing the same old thing? Did you ever really want to learn something somebody else hadn't shown you first? *Do you know what I'm talking about Mark?* Do you understand? These corporations and the government, they want everybody to want to be what they want—eager consumers, loyal citizens. Nobody making trouble. They want people to watch HV or listen to viddisc. *They don't want people to think!* Mega's a fraud, Mark, It has beautiful trees and lush meadows, and the buildings are large and attractively constructed. Everything is lovely to look at, but everything stays the same."

Mark stared at Jessica. He had always loved Mega, loved its grassy hills and walkways. Nothing bad had ever happened in Mega. There were no surprises. Was that because people weren't thinking for themselves?

Jessica leaned forward to Mark. "Hey, I know *you* liked it there. It is peaceful, but peace is worthless if you don't know what it means. That's the danger of BCS, Mark. That's why we have to expose it. That's what my father had to do! My father used to work with one of the biggest companies in the electronics communications industry. He knows it in and out,

Mark. They used to distribute his records. He knows the people there, he knows things that he's not supposed to know. He knows what they've done with synthenization. He knows what the companies have planned for BCS. They're getting to the kids first, Mark. They're getting to the people who have the most to lose. Right now they have the government sold on BCS as a way to stop smoking, end violence, and reinforce good health care. They're testing it! You won't believe what they have next!"

Mark watched Jessica. She gazed out the window behind her, her face filled at once with determination and sorrow. He knew the secret now. He knew the puzzle. He remembered Wein back at the Youth Center. He remembered the way he had been staring off into space. They were using synthenization to affect the kids in Mega. It would take time, it would take money, but he understood what Jessica was saying. He knew then what nineteen years in Mega had been. They had made him docile with the comfort, the isolation, the HV.

Jessica looked at him warmly.

Mark returned the look. She was an attractive girl, but not in the way Mark was used to seeing. Jessica did not look like the girls on holovision. She looked comfortable with herself.

Jessica Star was not on display for anybody. She reminded him of the people in the Piper. She looked *real.*

He wanted to be that way. To be really alive. He suddenly understood Herbie much more than he ever had. He understood his friend's anger, his anxiety about Mega. "Jessica," Mark said softly, "I'm with you all the way."

"*All* the way?" she asked.

Mark nodded.

"Not so fast, Guts." She smiled. "You don't know what you're getting yourself into here."

"I know your father and my friend may have died for it. I know a whole town is threatened. A whole country! You need me, Jessica. You need somebody who can help."

"I haven't even told you the secret yet! The secret of the log book!"

Mark was shocked. "The secret? Isn't the secret what they're doing with BCS? With synthenization?"

"No, Mark, that's what my father was trying to fight," she said. "It wasn't the only reason why they wanted him."

Mark blinked. "You mean there's more?"

"More than you imagine."

"Tell me!"

"I don't think you want to hear this, Guts."

"Yes, I do."

"No, I don't think you can take any more shocks right now. I don't think I should tell you what you'll have to do if you go all the way with us. It's too much at one time, Mark. It's really too much. You need food and rest."

Mark clasped her shoulder. "I'm fine, Jessica. I've never felt better in my life! Tell me what it is, Jessica. Tell me the secret!"

She turned away from him and looked out the window once again. "My father wasn't just a musician, Mark. He was an inventor." She faced him again. "He made a discovery. An incredible discovery. My father learned how to travel time."

Mark gulped. He wasn't ready for that—not ready by a long shot.

Then Jessica clasped *his* shoulder. "That's what you're going to have to do if you go all the way with us. You're going to have to travel time."

CHAPTER SEVEN

Mark had wanted to know more, but with dusk closing in, Jessica had felt they ought to get moving. She promised him an explanation later.

That evening they left the apartment, moving quickly through the back streets toward the industrial section of South Philadelphia. Just short of the area where the factories began, they went down the side alley of a large red brick building, and through a rusty back door. Inside, she led him through the darkness to a metal stairway. They climbed it to the top where there was another door.

The pair moved through it, stepping into a large dark room, filled with rows of huge machines covered by sheets. They moved forward, slowly.

"Sorry for the secrecy, Mark, but my father told me never to stay too long in one place when danger is hot. That's why they were able to get Herbie. They had a chance to learn his routine. My father and I have over thirty abandoned buildings staked out throughout the city. We can use any of them at a moment's notice for a meeting with the... others."

Mark nodded. She had explained about the others who knew of the synthenization plan and had formed a network to fight it.

As they made their way through yet another door, she said, "You would have liked my father, and his music. Oh, Mark, he was such an incredible guitarist. Back in the '50's, on the old Phillies label, all of his records were big sellers. You see, dad could play the electric guitar so well, mainly because he understood it. He knew what he could ask it to do.

"He was an innovator, he would gimmick guitars, creating new attachments and improvements all the time, but the record companies didn't care. Neither did the musical instrument supply houses. They said dad's devices were too futuristic, too impratical, too expensive.

"So dad pulled out, took all his money, and started to work on his own. He set up his own laboratory, and began experimenting with better and better types of guitars."

"This is all well and good, Jess," said Mark, "but what does it have to do with time traveling? That's what I really want to know."

"That's just the point. As he continued his study, dad discovered that there was an intimate relationship between time and music. I don't know what the first clue was he came across, but he followed it. He searched for the last fifteen years." She walked Mark past a large machine. "You'll understand all of this soon, Guts. I promise you."

Mark squeezed her hand. As she continued to lead him through the labyrinth of machinery, he answered, "Don't worry, I'll wait."

"You're a good survivor," she said. "There must be a lot more to you buried under the surface, Guts. A lot that still has to surface. The longer you're away from Mega, the more you'll grow."

They had come to the last door. She fitted another key in the lock, and opened it. After they were on the other side, she flipped a light switch giving Mark his first look at where he was. Being able to see it, however, still did not tell him what it was.

"This used to be a printing plant," said Jessica. "They made books, here. Magazines and newspapers, things like that."

"Why don't they use it anymore?"

"Companies make more money on HV. There's not as big a demand for books. Everything is being put on tape for us to look at, rather than read in our hands. Did you know restaurant menus used to be handed to you—that you just didn't go in and look at a computer terminal when you sat down to eat? Comics used to be drawn on paper, rather than being on HV. Oh, Guts,

there is so much that's changed. You used to look in a book for phone numbers."

"Wouldn't that be harder?" said Mark. "It seems it would take more time to look through a book full of phone numbers for the one you wanted than it does to punch in a request on the HV."

"That's true, but before, if you looked the number up and went out to a pay phone and called, nobody knew it. Now, they have records of every call you want to make."

"That's true! I never thought of that! Sure, it makes charging people for calls a snap—but it also helps them keep information on everybody. If you know you can't make a call from Mega without the government knowing, then you're practically. . . ."

"It all starts to add up, doesn't it, Guts?"

"It sure does."

Mark looked around the old printing plant. The roof was a massive overlay of glass and steel. The skylight admitted little light.

They were in the center of what used to be Philadelphia's industrial section.

"Jessica, why are we here? You said there were over thirty places you and your father could use as needed."

Jessica leaned next to one of the presses and said, "This building is open to us now, and is roughly halfway between the two places we are going tonight."

"Which are?"

"You're going to my dad's apartment. We need something from it. His guitar."

"Why?"

"My dad did everything he could with music. It was his defense. The guitar is the key which opens his lab. We need it to get to the time travel equipment."

"He keeps the guitar in his apartment?"

"He always did. I hope they haven't gotten to it yet."

"What are you going to be doing?"

"While you're getting the guitar, I'll be at the Philadelphia Mental Health Center on Chestnut Street. I'm hopefully going to bring back somebody who will be able to help us—somebody we need very much."

"Who?"

"His name is Manny Green. He's an old friend of my father's. Oh, I can't tell you now! By the time I get there, visiting hours will be almost over. We have to get ready."

"So, I go get the guitar, and you get this guy from the mental health hospital. Is he all right?"

"Basically." Jessica smiled. "We'll all meet back here."

"Ah, that way, if something happens to one of us, or if one of us is followed, the other one doesn't necessarily get caught too. Right?"

"That was my thinking."

Mark smiled now. He knew he was changing, improving.

"Guts, I know you've been taking a lot on faith lately, but just trust me this much further. After we get back tonight, we'll be going straight to dad's lab to get started. All right?"

"All right. Your dad sure taught you a lot, didn't he?"

"He tried."

"At least he taught you to use his machinery. That means we have a chance, doesn't it?"

Jessica nodded. "A crazy chance, but a chance still." She had taken the log book from Mark and hidden it safely in a drawer in one of the printing presses.

"What do you mean?" asked Mark.

She frowned. "I mean that if we can't find the proof he hid in the past, we're in big trouble."

"Proof. . . in the past?"

"Look, I better tell you this now. . . just in the event something happens to me. My dad hid all his evidence about BCS in the past."

"Do you know where? I mean, you don't have any idea?"

"I know that it's in the '50's."

"That's it?! Just *the '50's?* Ten years?!"

"No. It's specifically between 1952 and 1958."

"Seven years? That's a bit easier." Mark was upset.

"Easier?" Jessica ran her hand through her hair nervously. "My dad isn't the person who took the stuff back, Mark!"

"Who did? Did *you?*"

"No. You see, dad wanted to hide the stuff in the '50's. He said he had the perfect place. But a person can't go back to a time in which he has already lived. Since dad was alive in the '50's, then someone else had to take it back."

"*Herbie?*"

"Yes."

"Fantastic. He never said a word about it."

Jessica started to walk toward the exit. "Time to go, Mark. We'll talk later. Dad lives at *1456 Pine Street.* Apartment *3-F.* Remember?"

"I memorized it already."

"Keep an eye out for Munroe."

Mark nodded. They headed down toward the street.

Mark spent little more than half an hour walking to David Star's apartment. It was unguarded, except for a doorman. A trap? He knew one way to find out. Walking up to the front door, he addressed the diminutive doorman. "Is this 1456 Pine?"

"Yes, may I help you?"

"You already have. I'm supposed to pick up a package for Special Forces Agent Bender."

"I don't know anything about a package."

"You're not supposed to know. I'll just go up and get it. You stay here." He headed inside, but the doorman grabbed his arm. "You can't just walk in there! Get out!"

Mark ignored him and pulled in the heavy glass door.

"Hey!" The man grabbed his collar.

Mark shook the puffy-faced doorman off. Slipping through the lobby door, he raced inside and rushed for an elevator.

"*Police! Police!!*"

He'd done it again.

The elevator seemed to be on an upper floor. Mark saw a red hall light and headed toward it. There was a staircase. Grabbing a railing, he took the steps three at a time, heading for the third floor. Once upstairs, Mark searched quickly for the door to Star's apartment.

He grabbed the knob to apartment 3-F. It was locked. Stepping back, he ran forward and threw himself against the door. It hardly budged. Mark slammed himself against it again. The third time he heard the jamb crack. The fourth time he saw the crack spread. The fifth time he fell inside as the door flopped open. Staggering, he walked through the apartment and clicked on a light. Clothing and books were strewn about haphazardly. The mattress had been torn open, drawers emptied on the floor, the closet ransacked.

He glanced into the next room. The guitar hung at an angle on the far wall, as if it had been taken down and hung up again. He hurried toward it.

In the hall outside, the doorman was approaching. He had company. Munroe's men.

"He's in there! This time we have him!" The men burst into the apartment with a speed to match their determination.

"Gutstein!" shouted one of them. "Don't move!" He waited. There was no reply.

The three agents rushed into the bedroom. Empty but—*the guitar was missing!* Jones stared at the large glass windows of the room. Silently he motioned for another agent to open them. As he did, Jones stepped forward, his identifier ready.

"Now!"

Jones stuck his head out the window and in the next second he felt the heavy fiberglass case of David Star's guitar on his neck.

"Bye!" Gutstein jumped from the window ledge, three flights below him. "Too close!" he thought, as he dropped the guitar to the ground, before he landed. A laserblast burned through his shirt as he touched down. He rolled on the ground in the yard below Star's window, picked up the guitar, and kept running until he reached Chestnut Street. There, he waved madly with the guitar for a taxi. Five minutes later he was on his way back to South Philly.

Jessica had arrived at the Mental Health Center at nearly the same time Mark had reached her father's apartment building. Her entry was easier. The middle-aged woman at the reception desk was a familiar face. "Why, Ms. Star. So nice to see you again! Visiting hours are almost over, you know."

"I know. I just want to drop in and say hello."

"Here to visit Mr. Green, aren't you?" Jessica smiled disarmingly. "I know I have only ten minutes," she said, "but it

means so much to Manny if I come by, and I haven't been here in so long. It's all right, isn't it?"

"Oh, I suppose so. It *is* still visiting hours, after all. You can go back to the ward. Mr. Gunnder is on duty. He'll take you back."

"Thank you, Evelyn."

"Oh, that's all right. Don't you worry. I'm just glad that there is somebody to visit with Mr. Green. I feel so sorry for him. I mean, there are a lot of people who belong here, to be sure, but Mr. Green is so friendly, so alive—and such a tease. Why, if the doctors didn't say so, a body would never even know he was crazy. Oh, I'm rambling again! I'm sorry! You'll run out of time."

Jessica smiled. "Thank you, Evelyn."

"Go on now, I'll see you when you come out."

Jessica reached Gunnder's desk just as he was hanging up the phone. An older man, Jessica assumed he was in his late forties. He stood up as she approached, and said, "Here to see Mr. Green?"

"Yes, Mr. Gunnder."

Gunnder began to ramble about rules and regulations and "these damn fool hospital doctors" while they walked back through the ward. They strolled through the green corridors, heels clicking against the hard tiles.

When they got to Manny Green's room, Gunnder opened the door for Jessica. "Manny, are you home?"

"Don't know where else I'd be, Gunnder."

"You got you a visitor, Manny."

Manny Green was a very old black man. He was tall and thin, with sharp, intelligent brown eyes, and a tight skull cap of silver hair covering his head. He wore a small salt and pepper goatee, which he had always considered "artsy." Jessica walked past him, saying hello, and took a seat. Gunnder just leaned in to say "hello" to Manny and remind the pair they only had a few minutes to talk. He never got the chance. Jessica caught hold of Gunnder's arm and pulled him into the room. Before Gunnder could react, Manny jabbed him with a hypodermic needle. Jessica held him down, then clamped a hand over Gunnder's mouth for several seconds. Two minutes later Gunnder was unconscious.

"*Manny, are you all right?*" said Jessica as they dragged the body to Manny's bed.

"Never felt better." The old black man grinned.

"Are you ready?"

"I been ready for years. Shoot, I'm ready. I'm done, I'm so ready."

"Then let's go."

Jessica and Manny stepped out into the hall. "You know this is crazy," Manny whispered.

"I'll take my chances," Jessica said. "We're all going underground after this anyway, so there isn't much sense in worrying about it."

"All right, but it's still a long way to the front door. As soon as somebody notices that Gunnder is missing. . . ."

Before Manny could finish his sentence, the PA system started blaring. "*Manny Green. Manny Green. Go to a correction box. Manny Green. Manny Green. Go to a correction box. You have ten seconds.*"

Manny grabbed Jessica's hand, pulling her along.

"Manny, what is it?"

"Run. They know I'm gone. If I don't lock myself in one of those steel phone booths, they're going to turn on the holos."

They ran. They had covered half the distance to the front desk when the holos hit. In ten seconds their senses were assaulted. "Manny," shouted Jessica, "what's happening?"

"Close your eyes, darlin', put your fingers in your ears, close your mouth, and go where I pull you."

The hallway was equipped with a sensory disrupter, used to confuse troublesome or escaping prisoners. Holographic distortions replaced the long hospital walls. Swaying lines, floating patterns, and sight bafflers continued to appear around them. The walls themselves were charged with a pulse of electric current to discourage those trying to follow the real wall.

Manny shut his eyes, ignoring the noise around him, falling object sounds, shrieks, bizzare music, and dozens of other repeated audial cues all trying to get him to open his eyes. He forced himself to keep them tightly shut. He knew what he would see if he did not. He had traveled this hallway thousands of times in his years of confinement and had spent hours memorizing their labyrinthine turns to his room. Now it had to pay off for him, for Star's daughter.

Suddenly a cluster of security guards rushed at them from the hospital lobby. The first, a tall man with a stunner, shouted loudly, "Break up! I'll get the girl—ya take the old man."

"Jessica," Manny whispered. "Be careful. He's got a stunner—won't cut you, but it'll make you feel weak."

"Don't rush—they're in holo-shock from the hallway." The man with the stunner approached Jessica in the lobby.

Manny ran for cover, looking for a way to outwit the men.

The man with the stunner cornered Jessica, and then caught her with a swift slip of his arms. He didn't realize that Jessica had kept her eyes shut to the holographic assault.

Jessica broke the wrist-lock the man had on her, and swung her arm upward, digging her fingers into his throat. As he released her shoulder to pull her hand away, she made a fist which she sank deep into his abdomen. She felt something drop to the floor.

"Grab her!"

Jessica took a chance and opened her eyes. The security men in their striped costumes were faintly visible to her, blending into the holograph, but still perceptible. As another came toward her, she kicked upward, sending him tottering backwards. Another dropped the strait jacket he was holding and dove for her. Stepping back quickly, she picked up the injured guard's stunner.

Manny heard the sounds of lasers, the crashing noise of sliding rock, and all the others produced by the holographs. He knew security men with protective headgear would be searching the halls for them. After seeing that Jessica had disabled her attackers, Manny ran across the room to her side. With one hand grasping Jessica's belt, and the other feeling the wall, Manny then continued guiding them toward the front exit. He listened to the sound of his heels on the tile. Then, suddenly, Manny felt the front hall's carpet beneath his feet.

"Child, we're in the lobby! Just a couple of minutes. . . ."

There was a flash of light from the exit doors—security guards were rushing in after them! The natural spotlights outside flooded the lobby hall and Manny saw four men—three armed,

the last with a laser stunner, all helmeted to protect them from the holograms. Then the door closed again and they were back in the black nightmare again.

Jessica gained the ground she needed. As the man closed on her, she brought her knee up, crashing it into his jaw. Although she ruined his tackle, his force propelled him into her, sending the pair rolling across the floor in a tangle of thrashing arms and legs.

In the meantime, Manny had managed to keep busy without getting himself hurt. Swinging backwards, he kicked his captor in the leg. The man loosened his grip for a second, giving Manny the freedom he needed to break away from him. Another closed on him, but was cut off by a laser blast.

Manny looked to his right and saw Jessica. She was waving a laser stunner that she had picked up in a struggle with the first security guard. She could hardly tell where her first blast had hit the wall. She knew the weapon was incapable of seriously injuring anybody and turned around quickly in the lobby hall yelling, "Manny!"

"I'm down, darlin', go ahead!" came a voice from the corner of the hall. Manny hid behind a desk.

Jessica slid the control on the laser stunner forward and fired quickly in three directions.

"Dive!" yelled one of the guards. "She's crazy!"

"Not crazy!" said Jessica in the confusion. She heard two guards groaning over the din of the security system. "Drop your helmets on the ground!"

She could not be sure, due to the holographic disorientation in use, but she thought she saw two guards reaching up for their protectors.

"Hurry!" she yelled. It would take them a few minutes to get as accommodated to the patterns with their helmets off their heads.

"Now don't move," she added. "Manny! Can you get over here and get two of the helmets?"

Jessica heard footsteps coming toward her. Then she felt Manny's hand on her shoulder.

"Here, put this on tight!"

She felt the helmet and put it over her head as Manny kept the laser facing the guards.

"All right!" she whispered, "let's get out!"

Seeing the door of the large carpeted hall through their helmets, they rushed toward it, Jessica again firing the laser stunner in the direction of the guards. Two were buckled up in pain, a third dodged a shot, and the fourth had already hit the floor.

Manny tugged at her shoulder. "C'mon, Jess. Let's get our tails out of here."

Jessica agreed. She was scared and needed no prompting. Once outside, they threw the helmets and the laser pistol into the shrubs. They ran as quickly as they could into the long shadows of a nearby sidestreet.

Jessica and Manny arrived at the printing press an hour after Mark. They found him waiting in the shadows outside the old building in the alley.

"You got it?" asked Jessica.

Mark nodded back toward the shadows. "It's over there. Wasn't easy. Munroe's agents caught me just as I was jumping out the window."

"The *window?*" asked Jessica. "Dad's apartment is on the third floor!"

Mark smiled sheepishly. "I'm a good jumper."

Manny watched him. "Good jumper, huh? You're as crazy as I am."

"You're Matty?"

The man shook his head. "The handle is *Manny,* Manny Green, on the scene, never mean and not obscene."

Mark looked baffled.

Jessica smiled and said, "He likes you."

Mark grinned. "Oh, then, hello Mr. Green! To meet you is keen, and if you like what you've seen, shake hands with a Mark called Gutstein." Mark extended his hand.

Manny shook it. "Hey, you're all right, boy. That's fast, damn fast. I like ya, kid."

"That's something that doesn't happen every day," said Jessica. "Count yourself among a very privileged few with those words, Guts."

"Watch it, Jess. You're going to make me sound like some kind of snob."

"You aren't?"

Manny clapped his hands together. "Darlin', I just have good taste! Enough of me, though. Where's your dad?"

Jessica looked at Mark, then at Manny. "He's missing," she answered. "Been missing since last night. I didn't want to tell you on the way here. I have to carry out his plans alone, Manny. Will you still help me?"

Manny looked angry. "What sort of question is that, Jessica! You ain't alone. You have me and this kid from New Town. You have nothing to worry about, you hear me? We're gonna help you and we're gonna find your father!"

Jessica smiled faintly. "I'm sure the Special Forces took him. Same way they took Herbie."

"The fat kid you were telling me about a few months ago?"

"Yes, dad's courier." Jessica looked around warily. "Look, we shouldn't stand around here. There may be an unexpected guard or even a tracer from the hospital."

"I can get the book," said Mark.

"We'll all come," answered Jessica. "There's a lot to explain to Manny."

Manny shook his head. "Hey, now's not the time for Twenty Questions. There's something I want to know right now, before any more running around gets started. I'm sixty years old, y'know. I have my needs."

Jessica smiled. "There's a bathroom at my father's lab. That's where we're going, Manny."

"I don't mean that, darlin'. I want to know when I'm going to get a chance to eat."

CHAPTER EIGHT

The building waited before them. To Mark, it was a monstrous stone and steel construct towering out of the smaller buildings around it. It had a minimum of windows, and those were barred. As the trio made their way through the darkness, Mark realized that from his position, he had mistakenly thought there was only one tower. Now he could see that there were four, with sweeping expanses of smaller buildings going in many directions on the ground.

Mark asked Jessica, "Just what is this place, anyway? It looks like it's abandoned."

"It's an old government lab complex. They abandoned these research facilities a number of years back. When they moved out, my dad moved in."

"Didn't they leave any monitors to check for stuff like that? Or guards, or something?" asked Manny. "You'd think they would."

"Dad thought so, too, but they didn't. The government is like that."

"So they just let all of this sit here?" asked Mark.

"Oh, they send an inspector every other month, but all he does is make sure the locks are all in place, and that the fences haven't been fooled with, stuff like that."

Mark stood looking at the deserted acres of buildings. Suddenly a thought came to him. "If this guy comes to check everything, how can we break in? Won't he know?"

"We don't have to break in, Guts," answered Jessica. "Why not?"

"We have a key."

"Oh, you mean the guitar."

"No, that's for later."

"C'mon, Guts. The lady's too slick," added Manny. "I gave up trying to get anything on her long ago."

Mark shrugged his shoulders and joined in step as the others started toward the buildings. They stopped at a gateway. Using her flashlight, Jessica examined the bottom of the lock which held it shut. After a few seconds, she let it drop back into place. Before Mark could ask, she explained, "They're numbered. Each lock has a different key. We have a key for lock 2384. Each time he comes, the inspector likes to jumble the locks around. His idea of being tricky, I guess. We just have to find the right one, that's all."

Three gates later, they found it. After Jessica opened the lock and the others were inside, she slipped her hands through the cyclone fence's holes, and snapped the lock back into place. "Okay, men, straight ahead."

Although Jessica had assured them both that the place was safe, Mark and Manny were still nervous about sneaking through the night onto government property. Once inside, they felt relieved.

"It's not that I don't believe you, Jess, but it's still a little nerve-tickling to be scraping around in the man's backyard. If you can catch my drift."

"No offense taken, Manny. Really, I get the feeling that something is wrong, no matter how many times I've been here myself, so don't feel bad."

Mark and Manny joked as Jessica led them to the part of the installation which her father had taken over years earlier. It was in the heart of the complex. The government had been experimenting along many of the same lines that he had there. Then, suddenly, they came to a door whose lock had been slightly altered. Jessica said, "This is it."

"Well, let's go. What are we waiting for?"

"Don't you remember, Guts? I told you, the guitar opens the door."

"Well," said Mark, handing her the guitar, "here you go."

"I can't do it. You have to play the right chords to open the door. Elsewise the entire lab gets blown sky high."

Mark stammered, "Bu—but, I can't play a guitar."

"No," said Manny, "maybe not. But I can."

Mark handed the instrument to the black man. Manny fingered the strings, tuning them in order. "A Fender Stratocaster. Nice piece of fiberglass you got here." Manny tested the strings. Their response made Manny smile. He was ready. "Okay, what's the sound?"

"Six notes," answered Jessica. "G, G, C, A, A, C. Play it twice. That opens the door."

"All right. Show me where to plug this baby in, and I'm ready to roll."

"You don't plug it in. You play it just like that."

"You not goin' to hear much."

"That was dad's idea. Just play it like an acoustic—that's the correct level for the lock."

"Okay, you the boss. Stand back, folks. The scene is about to be made." Manny raised his hand to play the set Jessica had given him, but she stopped him. "What?" he asked.

"The key has to be in the lock." She inserted the key, turned it halfway. "It's ready. You have thirty seconds."

"Shoot," sighed Manny. He plucked out the twelve chords in half as many seconds. "I'm already done."

"Show-off." Jessica laughed. Mark sighed. As they went through the now-deactivated door, Jessica waved her hand in a sweeping motion.

"Welcome to the lab, Guts." As Mark passed her, he saw the girl's expression turn sour, as if she had suddenly remembered her father would not be there this time to greet them.

The walls were smoothed concrete. The laboratory was not a large one, but it was fully equipped, both with federal issue supplies and Star's extras. Many rows of amplifiers, consoles, and computers lined the walls, and filled much of the space in between. In the center of the room was a wooden platform. Mark, Manny, and Jessica walked across the carpeted floor and sat down upon it.

"Well, what's for dinner?"

"The kitchen is over there."

"Thank you, ma'am. Thank you." Manny followed Jessica's pointing finger to the small kitchen area. It was only a hot plate and a storeroom stuffed with boxes of canned goods. Manny sat down on one of the cots in the corner and began opening some canned vegetables.

In the meantime, Mark followed Jessica to one of the consoles. When she stopped before one, he asked her, "All right. We've come as far as we can. You made me a promise. I think now is as good a time as any for me to collect."

"You're right. It is time."

They were alone in David Star's electronics lab. Manny had gone to sleep in the back room, and so Jessica quietly started her lesson with Mark.

"I didn't want to talk in front of Manny, Mark, but the longer we stay here, the less safe we are."

"Huh?"

"Manny's a dear old friend of my father. He can teach you what you need to know, just as my father taught Herbie."

"About time travel?

"No, other things, things related to it. You'll find out later. I'm going to start explaining what my father explained to me a few years ago. It's complicated but I'm going to make it as simple as possible for you. I know you're smart; you've proved it. You're not a Megadrone. You've got to think fast, Mark, faster than you've ever thought in the past."

Mark nodded. He thought about the Cheeser's advice, those very words, and then he thought about his parents, worried and isolated from him.

"Jessica," he said softly, "if I go through with it, if I do what you want me to do—will I—can I ever come back?"

Jessica smiled. "Herbie did. More than once. When you come back, things may even have been cleared up. You might be able to go home. We might have found my father—and Herbie, too!"

Mark looked at Jessica. She was frightened, but confident. He respected her as if she were twenty years his senior. He wondered if other young people outside of Mega were the same as Jessica. Were they all so much more educated, self-assured than he?

No, he thought, Jessica's exceptional; she's been trusted with her father's plans, she has a goal, she. . . .

"Jessica," Mark asked, "why don't you go back in time instead of me?"

"I have to find my father, Mark. I have to take care of what he started. If he's alive—I hope, *oh,* I hope he's alive—then he's going to need me even more than he has in the past."

"All right, then, we'd better get started."

Jessica pulled down a screen from above the platform, then sat down behind the console with Mark.

"Watch," she said.

She slid a switch on the console and a videotape camera descended from the ceiling.

"Wow," said Mark.

"You're Jewish, aren't you Mark?" asked Jessica.

"How'd you know?"

"With a name like Gutstein?"

"Oh," Mark smiled.

"Besides, so am I."

"Really?"

"Don't look so surprised. There are a lot of us in Philadelphia."

"Why'd you ask?

"I was thinking of Einstein."

"I don't think I'm as smart as Albert Einstein, Jessica."

Jessica giggled. "No, Mark, I was thinking about my father's work. He wasn't as smart as Einstein, either, but his work owes a lot to the old professor's theories."

A picture of an atom came up on the screen.

"My father prepared this tape for Herbie, but Herbie really didn't need it."

"I think I do," said Mark. "I may be a fast learner, but I'm not a physics major. If you're gonna teach me about Einstein then. . . ."

"You're going to learn and learn it fast, Mark. Now listen."

David Star's voice blared out of one of the speakers. Jessica jumped, then adjusted the sliding switch for volume.

"This is a theory of time," said the tape. *"Please look at the atom on the screen."* Mark looked; the atom was vibrating, like in an animated cartoon.

"When you heat an atom, it vibrates at a specific wavelength."
Mark looked at the screen and saw a wavy up and down pattern, like a roller coaster, trailing behind the atom.

"A wavelength is the distance between the high points on the pattern you see."
A line between the peaks of the roller-coaster pattern came on the screen.

"About ten years ago, the United Nations agreed to measure distance, normal distance, such as meters and miles, in terms of the time it takes for an atom to vibrate and length of a wavelength equal to the distance involved. If you want to know how long a meter really is, you find out how long it takes for an atom to travel its wavelength the distance of a meter."
Jessica looked at Mark and put the tape on hold. "Do you understand that, Mark?"

"I think so—what your father is saying is that length can be measured in terms of the time it takes for an atom to move a certain distance. That distance is called wavelength, isn't it?"

Jessica beamed. "Terrific! I could kiss you!"

Mark blushed.

She slid the switch and the picture continued.

"Now what if human beings could travel wavelengths?"
A picture of a man in silhouette appeared on the screen.

"What if a man could do what that atom did? It wouldn't be easy. Atoms vibrate to travel and to vibrate they must be heated. If you heated a man, he'd die."
The picture changed to show the silhouette standing next to an electronic generator.

"There are other ways to make a person vibrate, however. You can shoot him through with electricity."
Mark laughed as the silhouette was given a jolt.

"Unfortunately, that would either kill him or shock him."
On the screen, the generator was replaced with a picture of an electric guitar.

"You can also expose a person to the vibrations of an electronic instrument. The high frequencies would make him vibrate."

The screen showed the frequency lines flowing from the instrument to the silhouette.

"It wouldn't be enough to send a man vibrating through time, however. For that he'd have to vibrate extremely fast, and that would probably kill him."

Mark looked warily at Jessica. "You father did come up with an answer, didn't he?"

She nodded. "Watch."

Mark concentrated on the screen. The simple silhouette of the man had become detailed, filled with little lines, like a map of rivers.

"Throughout your body are tiny neurons. They carry electronic impulses to and from various parts of your body, including your brain. Neurons never quite touch. The messages that they carry jump from the end of one neuron to another."

A close-up of a neuron appeared on the screen.

"Watch this," said Jessica, "it's a key to understanding dad's theory."

Mark saw a picture of a single neuron appear on the screen.

"A neuron has three main parts: the dendrite (receivers), the cell body (containing a nucleus), and an axon (which sends signals received by dendrites to other cells). The axon is what we are concerned with here, for in the axons, an electric potential exists.

"There are electronic charges in our axons."

The screen dissolved into a picture of an electronic recording—a picture of lines a lot like those used to detect earthquakes.

"The impulses that run through our axons can be measured. All impulses from the same neuron have the same length and voltage. Yet the frequency, the number of crests produced by an impulse in a second, can vary depending on the length of the strength of an impulse. The stronger the impulse, the higher the frequency.

"If we can increase the frequency of the impulses without hurting a person, we can in theory make him 'vibrate.' Since the voltage and length of time of the impulses are consistent, then we can affect those same neuron's wavelengths without changing

their structure. In effect, we can make the body's neurons function on a different scale of time.

"If the body is vibrating at the same time as the frequency of the axon impulse is amplified, then in theory a person can 'vibrate' into time without destroying himself."

Mark looked at Jessica. "What can make the body vibrate and also change the frequency of the axom impulses?"

Jessica nodded. "It's *axon*, Mark, and I'm glad you understood enough to ask."

She slid the switch from the videotape into the off position and stood up from the console. Proceeding over to the northern wall of the lab, she pressed a panel in the wall and a tiny section whirred open. Jessica removed something and returned to Mark.

In her hand were a set of thin, shiny silver bars.

"What are they?"

Jessica smiled. "They amplify—raise—the frequency of the impulses that run through our axons."

She handed them to Mark. "Now wait a minute while I get something else."

She headed into a storage closet and returned with an electric guitar of fiberglass design.

"We already have a guitar," said Mark.

Jessica shook her head. "Not like this!"

She removed a plate on the back. There was an elaborate pattern of wiring, over 5,000 circuits visible to the eye.

"Wow. What's it for, Jessica?"

"It's the partner to the bars. It can affect your body's ability to vibrate. Amplify it. Together with the bars, it can be used to go back through time."

"Together?"

"The bars amplify the electronic impulses in your neurons. The guitar, when used properly, causes your body to vibrate. The bars protect your body by harnessing the electronic impulses in your nervous system and modulating them to protect your body and reaction to the guitar. By playing the guitar at certain frequencies, you will be able to determine the length of time you will travel. This guitar rechannels and amplifies its sound to cause your body to vibrate."

"How do the bars work?"

"Easy," said Jessica. "Like magnets. They're attracted to the electromagnetic energy in your body. You just hold them in front of you and concentrate. Here, open your shirt and hold these near your chest."

Mark obeyed.

Holding the bars in front of his shirt, he concentrated on pulling them toward him.

A minute later, they did.

"Wow!"

The bars were adhering to his chest.

Jessica clapped her hands. "We're on our way, Guts. We're on our way!"

"You two were sure up late last night." Mark opened his eyes. He had fallen asleep on the wooden platform in the center of the room. He saw Manny standing in front of him. The old man held a knife in one hand and a loaf of bread in the other. "You look to be ready for a little breakfast, unless I miss my guess."

"No, you got it right on with that one. I'm hungry, all right."

"Shoot, I wonder why. You been working day and night with Jess to get ready. She's been teachin' you everything she knows about this stuff. You've been practicing the guitar and learning about time traveling, and nothing else."

"Well, I have to get ready."

"You realize how long you've been gettin' ready?"

"About a week now."

"Boy, you should pay more attention to things. I know we don't have the sun and the moon in here to tell us day from night, but don't you ever look at your watch?"

"What'd you mean, Manny?"

"We've been here almost two weeks now."

"Two weeks?" he said incredulously.

"Straight up, son. And you ain't had a decent meal the whole time. So just follow along. You and I are going to do a little cooking, and you and that insane little girl are going to sit down and have something worth eating for once. You kids, you never think about your health. Just cram anything into you and keep

106

running along, never think about nutrition, or vitamins, just eat the first thing you can find. . . ."

Mark smiled. Manny had a way of running along, cramming all his sentences one after another, that Mark liked. He knew the old man was sharp; he was not making fun of him. He enjoyed Manny's company. He wanted to know more about him. He wanted to know one thing especially. Trying to be tactful, Mark asked the older man, "Manny, you didn't belong in the Mental Health Center. How'd you end up in there, anyway? Jessica hasn't had a minute to explain it."

"Oh, a while back, I started helping Jessica's daddy with his time work and all. Well, to get some of the equipment that's in here now, we had to go to some of the big record companies. David, he went to some of his old friends, guys from the old days when we were both working under the Spector label. . . ."

"The old Phillies label?"

"Yep. Phil brought it back in the early '80's when he started recording tracks for release with David. That's when the trouble started with BCS. Research. Disco had been rolling hot for about six years and music had been getting more and more formularized and electronic. Used to be instrumentals were used as bridges for singers."

"Bridges?"

"You know, between lyrics and chorus and things like that."

Mark nodded. "Like a guitar in David Star's songs?"

"Yes, he'd use guitar bridges a lot. At any rate, disco sort of turned things around—instrumental sections became as important or more important than a lot of the singing. People wanted to dance to a beat. Many corporations at that time had started doing market research—y'know, finding out what sells— because there were so many songs that sounded alike, they were having trouble deciding which to push. A crazy situation.

"It was when they got the results of the market research— that told them how the kids responded to the music—that some people started to get the idea that they could influence the kids directly with the music. David and I tripped up on some of the BCS plans a long time ago and we've been working against it ever since."

"You've been in a mental hospital, Manny. How could you help?"

"Easy, kid. I took a lot of the rap. The government could pin certain stuff on either me—or David—but not both. We made sure to operate that way. Anything we did, we did alone. It was more important for Star to be on the outside. I still managed to do a little. My lawyer got me in there instead of jail by having me act crazy. That's not hard for a musician to do. I've seen the real thing too many times, Mark. I hope you never have to do the same thing."

"I'm really worried about David Star now that Jessica seems to have...."

"Did somebody ask for me?"

Jessica stood outside the small bedroom. She was smiling.

"Oh, good morning, Jess. I didn't even hear you coming.

"You weren't supposed to hear me coming. I'm no thundering elephant. I make a graceful entrance." "That you do," Mark agreed with a tone to his voice which made the girl blush slightly. As the trio began to chatter, Jessica brought three plates to the table. While she spread the silverware and glasses, Mark and Manny brought the food to the table. They talked about their progress during breakfast.

"So tell me. How's this boy taking to the guitar?"

"You tell him, Guts. How well do you think you're doing with your instant musical career?"

Mark looked at the girl with a modest grin on his face. "I don't know. I think I'm getting enough of it down so that I'll be able to work the machines. I hope, anyway."

"Oh, Guts, you're doing better than that."

"It doesn't sound much like any music I ever heard before. I don't mean the rock and roll; God, that stuff is great. Herbie was right. I just mean the way I play it. Face it, Mann, I'm a long way from being a muscian."

"The heck you are, boy," said Manny. "I've heard you. You're gettin' good. Real good. Truth to tell, I never saw anyone take to the guitar the way you have."

"No one ever had their life depending on learning to play the thing before," Mark reminded him.

"Yeah, but most people would just have to give it up for dead. You have a real gift for music, Guts, a capital S dose worth of soul. You really do. Sure, I know you're just running through exercises now, playing scales, worrying about whether or not you can stroke those machines into life and get back to do a little dance with the dinosaurs, but the short and simple is that I think you can."

Mark shrugged. "C'mon."

"I am not funning with you, Guts. You really have the touch. And I am going to bring it out. Jess . . . ?"

"Yes, Manny?"

"Would you say that Guts has mastered enough of the electronic end of all of this to get by for the moment?"

"I'll say more than that. He knows how to atune the bars to himself, he can play the right pace, he can manipulate everything better than I can. Outside of really going somewhere, he's as ready as he's going to be the day he leaves."

"Then, Guts," said Manny, "it is time for your real education to begin."

"What do you mean?"

"I mean, if you're going to slide yourself back to 1954, or somewhere thereabouts, you're going to need a little bit more training than what you've had from Jessica."

"I don't know what you mean."

"Listen, if you were going to another country, you'd read up on it, see what you could find out about the local customs, maybe learn some of the language, and stuff like that, right?

"Yeah, sure. But I'm not going to another country. I'm just going to Philadelphia."

"Philadelphia in the 1950's *was* a whole nuther country, Guts. It had its own language. People did things differently then. Don't you see? Listen, tell me, you're walking up the street. It's 1956. A girl sees you. Thinks you're top cut. She tells you that you're dreamy and wants you to go to the sock hop. What do you say?"

"Well, I. . . ."

"A couple of other dudes in black leather come up. They tell you that you just busted Eagle's turf, and if you don't rumble you're going to get iced. What are they talking about?"

"Maybe. . . , ah, I don't know."

"C'mon chicken, plant one on my kisser. I dare ya, I double-dog dare ya, chick-chick."

Mark listened to Manny, but didn't understand a word of what he was saying. Looking to Jessica for an answer, he saw that although she understood some of what Manny was saying, she did not really have much of an idea of what was going on. Manny clasped his hand on Mark's shoulder.

"A little confusing, eh, Guts? It should be. You go back there and talk to a guy on the street the way you do here, he's not going to know what you're saying. And you're not going to understand a lot of what he says either. You're going to have to *fit in.*"

Jessica interrupted. "Manny. . . ?"

"Yes, Jess?"

"Do you think it might help if you were to only talk like they did in the '50's around Guts?"

Manny stroked his chin with his long fingers. "Girl, that sounds like an A-okay idea. I'll start right now."

"We start right now?" asked Mark.

"You got it, boy-o. Of course, after all the years I've been bouncin' 'round this world, I may slide somethin' in from somewhere else, but I'm gonna try to give ya the best '50's education a man can get. You game?"

"Right on?"

Manny laughed. "About ten years off, and in the wrong direction, but we'll work on it. I promise you that. We shall overcome."

Thinking of the work in store for him, Mark rolled his eyes. Manny said, "Guts, you got the name for the times, I'll grant you that. I dunno what they're gonna think of you when you get back there, but you will be the baddest greaser Philadelphia ever saw when I get done with you."

Mark looked to Jessica for help. She only laughed. As he turned to Manny, the black man asked, "Any questions, Guts?"

Mark had only one word on his mind. "Greaser?"

"Yeah. You're goin' to become a greaser. Don't worry, boy, you gonna love it."

CHAPTER NINE

It was past midnight. Mark and Manny were still working. Sitting in the glow of the spotlight in the center stage, Manny strummed at the guitar around his neck.

"Quiz time."

"Lay it on me, Manny."

"1958, Texans were shook up. Why?"

"Ah, oil was first discovered?"

"No. It had something to do with Alaska."

"Oh yeah, Texas wasn't the biggest state anymore because that year Alaska became a state."

"That's better," said Manny. He continued, "There was one actor who was really big with the kids. Everything he said was cool. Who was he?"

"The *Rebel Without a Cause,* James Dean."

"The greatest ballplayer of the decade?"

"Willie Mays."

"What was rigged on TV?"

"The quiz shows."

"What were deepies?"

"3-D glasses. They made movies seem like they were coming out of the screen."

"Who was Uncle Milty?"

"He was a comic, a funny man."

"What were fallout shelters?"

"Where kids would go."

Manny looked at Mark with confusion. He asked, "What?"

"Yeah, where they'd go to fall out."

"You mean *hang out*. Fallout shelters kept you safe from atomic bombs."

Mark looked at Manny. He felt a bit foolish. "Sorry."

"Forget it. You ain't doin' all that bad. Let's keep goin'. Tell me, who was Joe McCarthy?"

"In what year?"

"1953."

"One of the strongest men in the country. If he called you a communist, you were through—whether it was true or not."

"How about in 1957?"

"He was a broken alcoholic. He died without any political power. But no one ever forgot him."

"Who was Harold Hill?"

"*The Music Man.*"

"What were hula hoops?"

"Stupid."

"No editorial comments." Manny grinned; then he paused, took a breath, and started again.

"Okay, now let's play name that tune. Here comes the notes. . . ."

Manny played a few introductory notes. Before he could get very far, Mark interrupted, "All Shook Up."

"Who's singing?"

"Elvis Presley."

"Who wrote it?"

"Otis Blackwell."

"Why?" asked Manny.

"He needed the dough."

"The what?"

"The bread," smiled Mark. "The scratch, the mazzuma, the lettuce, the coin, the cash. You remember, the long green."

"Money, huh?" Manny clapped his hands. "What's a greaser like you know about money?"

"Plenty."

"Where'd you get it?"

"I got it."

"How?"

"That's for me to know and for you to find out."

"How am I supposed to do that?"

"Don't know, and don't care. Catch the breeze, sleeze. Scram, scaddadle, take off."

"What you sayin' to me?"

"I'm sayin' make like the wind and blow."

"You know who I am?"

"I don't know, I don't care. I don't go, I don't scare. You don't point that beak of yours towards the southside and follow it, I'm gonna cut you four ways."

"Which four?"

"Long, deep, neat, and often."

Manny reached out and put his arm around Mark. Pulling him close, he hugged him, laughing. "Oh, Guts. You're ready. You're as ready as I can make you."

Mark hugged him back. "Do you mean it? Am I really ready to go back?"

Manny sighed. "In the time that crazy young woman's given us, you couldn't do much better. Two weeks is not much."

"Jessica's still trying to figure out the log book."

"Shoot. You might as well give up on that. There's nothing in that for you. How many times do you two have to read it?"

Mark argued, "I can't search six years worth of Philadelphia without a single clue. Not a year, or a place. Manny, all we have is David Star's past."

"That's nothing to belittle, kid!" Manny smiled. "Still, I sympathize with you and Jessica."

As he said it, Manny turned. Jessica was standing behind him, waving the log book at Mark.

"You found something," said Manny.

"You bet your sweet fuzzy face I did." Turning to Mark, she asked, "Quick, Guts. Where's the record from the log book?"

"It's over there, on the shelf."

Jessica ran to the corner he pointed at.

"What is it, Jessica?"

Jessica pulled the record from its sleeve. "This, this is it."

"Jess, honey," said Manny. "What is what?"

"Herbie *did* leave a message in the log book. We just didn't know where to look for it."

Jessica was still studying the record as Mark walked up to her. "Jessica. Will you explain what you're saying?"

"Herbie *was* eccentric, Mark. A good kid, but a bit eccentric. You know all those numbers on the last page of the log book?"

"Yeah—the record numbers?"

"Herbie had a code—simple but a code. Each number is a letter—A = 1, B = 2, and so on through. I realized it when the number was 26."

"What was the message?"

"It explains that he was worried about being caught. About the Special Forces people catching up with him. He says to get in touch with *you* if anything suspicious happened. He said you could be trusted."

Mark smiled proudly.

"He also says the clue to the recovery of my father's evidence is on the record in the log book."

"You've checked that record backward and forward," said Manny.

"Then we'll check it again!" snapped Mark. Manny was shocked. He had never seen Mark get angry before. "I'm sorry, Mann," apologized Mark. "It's just that if the message says that the record is the clue, then I want to check it out again. I mean, I'm going back in time. Whatever that clue is, I need it."

"Well, when you put it that way, what can I say? Let's get checkin'."

They did. They played the record ten times. Both sides. All they heard was David Star singing the same lyrics, every time. They tried the record under infra-red. They found nothing. They taped the record and then ran the tape backwards. There was no special message. Then Jessica tried playing it on a viddisc player. Although the record appeard to be a genuine 45 from the past, she thought Herbie or her father could have altered it. "If dad was really tricky, he might have coated the record and then coded it with computerized sound."

The words reminded Mark of Herbie's lessons.

"Old records worked by having a needle drag through their grooves," said Jessica. "Viddiscs play because a beam of laser light reads the message encoded on it in the form of microsopic

bumps. If there is a message to be laser-scanned on this disc, I'll know about it in a minute."

They waited. A laser beam in a viddisc player shined on the black vinyl, but its speakers produced neither music nor sound. They tried the other side. There was nothing. Mark refused to be discouraged.

"Let's play it at different speeds."

"We tried that."

"I mean backwards."

"I tried it at every possible speed."

Mark and Manny looked carefully at the 45.

"Maybe there's something under the label."

Jessica held the record at an angle at a light. "It doesn't look like it was taken off, but we'll do it anyway."

She soaked the labels from both sides in hot water. There were no messages.

"I don't know," said Jessica. "What do you think, Guts?"

Mark did not answer. Jessica turned around to find out why. "Mark?" she asked again. But there was still no response. Mark was gone. "Manny, where's Guts?"

"He left; went over to the next room."

"What's he doing in there?"

"Mostly likely he's thinking things out."

"What do you mean?"

"I mean if the kid has any sense at all, he's scared. I know if you were askin' me to climb up there and rock on back to nowhere, I'd be scared."

"Manny," asked Jessica, "do you think he might not go?"

The old man looked down at his friend's daughter. "Let's let him answer that. Okay?"

Jessica nodded. The pair watched the door to the next room, waiting for Mark to return.

Mark sat in the dim light of the small lab bedroom, staring at the wall. He had to go. He knew it. He also knew he was scared. He realized he could spend the rest of his life searching time for something he might never find. "God, I don't know what it looks like, how much of it there is, where it is, when it is." Mark rubbed his forehead. He remembered Herbie, possibly murdered, and Mazzari, caught by the Federal Special Forces men, and his parents, worried sick. And that he would have to hide out as long as the government was in control. Mark thought of the weeks he had spent with Jessica and Manny, of the good times, of all the fun they had had in between the learning and the preparing.

Mark looked at the leather jacket hanging on the door. He walked over to it. Taking it from the hook, he checked the fit. Manny had told him the leather jacket, with its huge pockets and many zippers, would be familiar in the '50's, especially around people into rock and roll. Mark reached for the tube of hair grease on the dresser.

"Greaser, huh? Okay, Manny, you got it."

A few minutes later, he went back into the main control room. Jessica stared at the black leather jacket. She looked up at Mark's slicked-down hair. As her eyes met his, she could see in them the answer to her question. He was ready to go.

Manny asked, "What you up to now, boy? Oh, you goin' to slide back to the past with a soggy record and solve everything, right?"

"I have to do something."

"I know you do, Guts. I know." The black man's voice was a whisper. "It's just. . . aw shoot, Guts. I don't want you to go now. You're people. You're my people. You're a part of me now. I just don't want to send you back there, not knowin' what you're lookin' for, not knowin' what's goin' on, with no protection, no direction, with no friends. . . ."

"I got friends, Manny. I got two of the best friends the world ever saw. I got everything,, man. C'mon. Dry those peepers, pops. I'm off. I've got to be gone." Suddenly Mark got very quiet. "You know I do."

"Don't you want something to eat first?" asked Jessica.

"Naw. I'll grab a shake an' dog when I hit 1950. Ya know. Balanced diet time an' all."

Jessica placed the record in the log book, and then handed it to Mark. "Here, you better take this. If the record leads you anywhere, you might need the book when you get there."

Mark saw a tear in her eye. Instead of taking the log book from her, he took her wrist. Pulling her to him, he said, "Jess.

Everything is going to be all right. I'm going to find out what they did to your dad, and Herbie, and what your dad had in mind. I'll find his proof, and the way he planned to use it.

"We're going to win, Jess."

The girl threw her arms around Mark's neck. He kissed her. He wanted to kiss her again, but he knew he had to leave. As he had many times already, Mark asked Jessica for reassurance.

"I'll be able to get back, won't I?"

"Herbie did."

"My parents, Jess. . . , if you could, I don't know, maybe you could write to them. Let them know I'm all right."

"I will."

"Are you and Manny going to be okay?"

"We should be. There's never any guarantee. We're going to see if we can get any more evidence. We'll be busy gathering facts when you get back. And remember, don't hop around too much."

"I know, we can't afford to take the chance that I might try and enter a time period I'm already in. I'll remember."

"It's important. You can't even mention being from the future to anyone."

"I understand. I'll get back."

"All right. Get the bars. Get your guitar. I'll meet you at the stage."

As the girl went to the main console, Mark climbed onto the platform. From the rear they both heard Manny's voice.

"You ain't playin' this one without me, Guts. Just give me a sec' to drag this bass up there. You are not goin' to leave without a send off straight from Manny Green's ten talented fingers. Understand?"

Mark smiled proudly. "I can dig it."

The pair tuned their instruments. Once his guitar was ready, Mark pulled the amplifier bars from his pocket. He held them in his hand, concentrating on them. Suddenly, they leapt from his hand to his chest.

Manny looked up. He was ready. Jessica nodded her head, biting her lip as she did. Mark gave them both the thumbs-up signal, and then started to play.

His hand strummed, creating a rippling beat which rapidly multiplied. Manny plucked at his bass from a safe distance. His long fingers coaxed the strings, pulling the duo together. Mark's hands blurred as they touched the strings, continually moving up and across the guitar, urging, pulling—demanding the sound. Manny followed with the precision of his years. He had been a bass player for twice the time Mark had been alive. His bass moaned, crying a background for Mark's own music. His hands were like spiders, leaping from place to place.

Jessica watched them from the console. She deftly moved switches on the flatbed, sweeping the area to confuse any Special Forces tracers that might be in operation.

She hoped her father would return before Mark. She hoped Mark would be able to find the clues. They had agreed on starting with 1956—the early days of rock and roll's popularity. Mark would travel forward in time from '56, associating with people from the music business in Philly—and if necessary, her father.

Jessica felt the familiar vibrations of the electronic equipment on stage. The process was starting to reach a crucial stage. Manny moved further away from Mark, off the platform toward the console. Mark continued to play; faster, louder, his body responding to the amplified frequencies of the guitar. The amplifiers were functioning correctly, compensating for the vibrations inside Mark's body by steadying the reactions of his nervous system.

"Ten!" Jessica shouted. "Keep playing, Mark!"

"Eight!" She glanced at Manny. He was watching the stage carefully. He would miss Mark's company, but more than that, he was worried about the young man's mission. The '50's were a different time and his mission was a dangerous job. Gutstein was still a young man with very little experience outside Mega. Manny had confidence in Mark, but he hoped it would be easier for Mark than he expected it to be.

"Six!" Mark was fading.

He was in pain. The stress on his nervous system had reached a critical stage.

"Four!" Jessica put her arm around Manny and watched Mark vanish into. . . .

"Two!" Manny waved tenderly at the phantom guitarist. "Goodbye, kid. See you soon."

"Zero." Jessica started to cry.

"What? Where am. . . oh, man!"

Mark was floating in a place without substance, where nothing he saw was recognizable. He found that he had no hands, no body. "I—I'm not here."

Mark did not understand what was happening to him. He felt himself moving forward at tremendous speed, and yet, there was no sensation of movement. "It's like being in a bubble in a river. I see things going by, and yet, I can't feel the motion."

Colors whirled around him. He passed through sections of light, swarming, splashes of brilliance, and although he was aware of them, he could not feel them. While he was among the colors, they were more real to him than his own legs or hands, but he was only a part of them for a moment, and then they were gone. The lights and colors would come back, repeatedly, bridged by periods of extreme darkness.

Then, suddenly, in the darkness, Mark found himself in the midst of a large group of black capsules, most of them traveling at an even faster rate than himself. They were all of the same size and dimensions, and all were made of the same glistening material. Mark had only a brief moment to register them, and then, they also were gone. Traveling in silence, he continued to move backward in time until finally he began to feel his body once more. I'm starting, he thought, I'm coming back. His left arm brushed against the guitar.

Mark was tumbling in what seemed like a downward direction. He closed his eyes, fighting the dizziness which had begun to assail him. When he opened them again, he was standing on a sidewalk in Philadelphia.

"I made it!" Mark jumped upward, shouting again, *"I made it!"*

Mark looked at the buildings around him. Everything was different from the way they had been in the '90's. Buildings he remembered were not yet where they belonged. Other, smaller,

buildings had taken their place. Older structures dotted the sides of the street. Mark looked at the people around him; everyone's clothing had changed. "It's like a city-wide costume party," he whispered.

Suddenly Mark noted that some people were staring back at him. Quickly he removed the bars from his chest and placed them in his left-hand jacket pocket. It was specially lined with a material which would protect them. The action did not stop the people from staring. Mark looked at his clothing, down at himself, but it seemed that everything was in order. He was fully dressed; his hair was firmly slicked into place.

"What are they staring at? Maybe it's the guitar."

Nobody had seen him arrive. A displacement field had seen to that, and yet. . . .

"Why are they pointing, and laughing?" Mark hurried down the street. He felt weak. He was confused as to why people found him amusing. Finally, at a street corner, the truth began to dawn on him. *This isn't it. It isn't like Manny said it would be.*

Mark observed the street again. There were little things out of place. There was a McDonald's restaurant, but there were no McDonald'ses in the '50's. "This is crazy," he said. "The clothes, that's why they're staring at me, the clothes aren't what they should be. All those women, they should be wearing dresses. All those men, wearing colored shirts, and funny shoes, this isn't what's supposed to be here."

Looking into the street, the cars he expected to see were not there. Where were the tail fins, hot rods?

Spotting a newsstand, he crossed the street. The clerk's eyes turned to Mark as he entered. Mark ignored the man, walked to the newspapers stacked against the wall. Picking one up, he found what he was looking for. Before he could catch himself, he blurted, "1976? It can't be 1976!"

"What'd you expect, Fonzie? It can't be the '50's forever, you know."

Mark felt the world closing in on him. He hadn't the faintest idea what to do. He ran from the newsstand, his guitar slamming into his jacket. He made it two blocks before he rounded a corner, blacked out, and crashed against the sidewalk.

"Hello?"

Mark groaned a response to the half-question. When he finished opening his eyes, he found himself lying on a red couch. It was a color which reminded him of apples. It was the color of the hair of the girl kneeling next to him.

"What time is it?"

"About 2:15."

"No. No, I mean when is it?"

The girl looked at him with a puzzled expression. "What do you mean?"

"Ah, I'm sorry." Mark glanced around the room. There was too much glass, too much chrome. The white rugs and walls contrasted against the deep black leather furniture. There were heavy draperies, reaching from the ceiling to the floor, and a scent in the air which Mark recognized from home.

"Some things never change," he guessed. Getting a hold of himself, he said, "I meant, *where* am I?"

"This is my place."

"Who are you?"

"I was wondering if you'd ever think to ask. My name is Chase, Barrie Chase."

Mark sat up, rubbing his face. He was still a bit dizzy. He flinched as he touched a patch of raw skin.

"You tore your face up when you fell. On the cement, you know?"

"How'd I get here?"

"Well, you passed out on the street outside. I brought you here."

"You did?" Mark said it with surprise. The girl did not appear to have the strength.

"I had a friend do the carrying, if that's what you mean. I'm not built for that kind of work."

"What do ya do?"

"I'm a disc jockey at WFUN. You know, the big sound in Philly."

Mark thought for a second. *Disc jockey? What was it? Manny told me. Oh yeah, radio announcers. . .DJ's.* Quickly, he said aloud. "You're a real DJ, huh?"

"You bet, the main vein. All the usual, 'Tune in, kids, Big Barrie is going to talk away the aches and pains all over your bodies with the latest music from Main Line to Camden. Now here's a new single from. . . .' Then you fill in some group's name and the title and *voila,* you're a disc jockey." She sat down next to him. "You've been getting all the answers. C'mon now, fair is fair. What's the name?"

"Me?"

"There's nobody else here."

"Mark Gutstein."

"This stretched out six feet of handsome hunk is named Mark Gutstein? Nothing better?"

"Those who know me call me Guts."

"Then Guts it is. So, as long as I'm still getting the answers, where'd you get the outfit, Guts? Are you in a street production of *Grease* or something?"

Mark stared at the girl. "Ah, no."

"You're not with Sha Na Na, are you?"

"Ah, naw. Not me." Mark didn't know what she meant.

"Well, why the rig?"

"Ya mean the clothes?" Mark was confused. They really did have another language. He knew that Jessica had told him not to give any hints. He also knew his knowledge of other time periods was limited. He could be comfortable in the future or the '50's, but it would be hard to fit in between those two periods. He knew what he had to do. To protect his friends, to protect himself, he would stay a greaser.

"Yeah," she answered, "the clothes. What's this getup all about, anyway?"

"Hey, it's just my style. A guy's got to be cool, you know?"

" 'Cool'? Nobody says 'cool' anymore. Just what are you? What do you do for a living, huh?"

"I hang out. Maybe I fix a car for a dude, if he's all right. I got my friends. There are ways to be taken care of if you're in need, babe. No problem."

Barrie was becoming annoyed at what she assumed was a put-on. "All right. Who put you up to this? Danny? Sid? Or one of those other clowns down at the station?"

"I don't know no Danny."

"You're a fan?"

"No, I ain't no fan. I'm just a guy. It's me and my guitar. You brought me in here, I didn't come lookin' for you, remember? Why'd you bring me up here, anyway?"

"I—I thought you looked interesting."

"Uh-huh, sure."

"That's right. Don't you sneer at me, you—you punk. I should have known better. I thought you were an actor, or a musician, or something. Not everybody runs around with a Fender Stratocaster."

"I got class."

Mark had to keep from smiling. The woman was getting angrier by the minute.

"Now, c'mon, Gutstein! What do you really do? You're a musician, huh?"

"I'm unemployed. Not much work around for greasers these days."

"You're a greaser, eh?" She said it lightly, smiling.

"Yeah. Gen-u-ine."

She laughed. "A '50's expert, huh?"

"I *am* the '50's. They're my home. Every day takes me a little bit closer."

"Ah! A neurotic! That I can sympathize with sufficiently."

Mark grinned. "You got any gum?"

"Gum? Gum? I'm talking about neurosis and you want spearmint?" Barrie laughed at the absurdity of the conversation. "Look, my original idea of getting you dropped in here was out of left field. You just looked different; I had to know who you were, are, I mean, it was an impulse. Now I have an idea. Listen, can you use a job?"

Mark thought quickly. He needed time. He knew he was not strong enough to make another time jump yet. He'd have to wait for a couple days to give his body a chance to rejuvenate. "Yeah, sure. I can use a job."

"Can you do this nostalgia thing well? I mean, can you really sell the '50's?"

"Faster than an Oldsmobile."

"Who started the Elegants?"

"You mean the Crescents?"

"No, the Elegants."

"Vito Picone started 'em in Staten Island, honey, but they called themselves the Crescents first."

"Maybe, Gutstein. Who did 'Speedo'?"

"The Cadillacs."

"Who founded Motown Records?"

"Berry Gordy."

"What year?"

" '56."

"Where?"

"Detroit. Where else but the Motor City, turkey?"

"Barrie will be sufficient. You really do act like a greaser."

"Top of the charts with a bullet. I'm leather coated, jeaned, mean, all man, and greased for action."

"You're also a creep, Gutstein, but you're cute."

Mark frowned. "What sort of work do you have in mind?"

"Well, there is a snag. Maybe I got your hopes up, too. The guitar's not for show, is it?"

Mark played a few Buddy Holly riffs. He was worried. After two weeks of practice, his repetoire included Buddy Holly, David Star, and a little Elvis. After that it was strictly r 'n' b improvisations, care of Manny Green and himself.

"My boss is looking for a gimmick," said Barrie, "for a shopping center opening. He doesn't know how to kick it off. He's supposed to line up the talent. Well, he has something to please the oldsters and the tinys, but he hasn't really found an angle to bring in the teens. You could be it."

"How do we find out?"

"We'll have to go down to see him. I'll go first, and if I can sell him on the idea, I'll take you down. Then you can sell him your pitch. This will work. You could walk in there and snap it right up. He's had a lot of trouble getting good acts, and he's desperate. If he doesn't have anyone by Friday, he has to give back the money the store's put up for the show."

"I take it he's not the kind of man who likes to do that sort of thing."

She grinned. "You take it correctly."

"So, when do we see him?"

"I'll run down there now. You go ahead and get a burger or something. There's nothing in my fridge. I'll meet you back in the lobby downstairs at six."

"Okay. Sure, I'll be here."

Barrie slung her shoulder bag back up into place, snapping it closed. As she and Mark went out into the hall, she said, "Listen, I'm sorry everything wasn't real smooth. . . I just. . . ."

"It's okay. I can dig it. I'll see you later."

As she waited for the elevator, she saw Mark checking a black hardcover book. It was the log book.

Mark turned his back on the girl and walked for the elevator.

"What's that?" Barrie asked.

"Just a book I'm holding for a friend. Wanted to check it, make sure it didn't get hurt when I fell. See," he pulled the 45 out, "there's a record back here. It's okay."

As he slid the record back into its sleeve, Barrie said, "What did you mean when you said you were going back to the '50's, Gutstein?"

"It's just my trip. I'm headed there. One of these days I'll make it."

Barrie kidded, "Any idea when you're leaving?"

Mark knew she was joking, and so he answered seriously, "It's just a matter of time."

CHAPTER TEN

Mark sat in the McDonald's he had seen earlier. Barrie's apartment building had turned out to be only a few doors away from it. Taking another bite from his Big Mac, he began to piece everything together that had happened to him since he had materialized in 1976.

It didn't make sense, he thought. Everything had been planned out to the last second—the guitar, the bars, even the time coordinated on their schedule. It had all worked for Herbie. He'd gone back and forth as David Star's courier without a problem. Why didn't it work for him? Could there have been some error on Jessica's part? Could she have forgotten something in her father's notes?

Mark bit into the wax edge of his cola cup. Could David Star have been hiding something from his own daughter to protect her?

No, Mark decided, he would have had to tell her. If Jessica didn't know how to operate the equipment in his absence, then the secret of time travel might be lost.

Maybe there was another explanation. What if it was all part of a plan? What if Star had altered the equipment before he disappeared? Perhaps for a reason that only he and Herbie understood? What if Herbie was supposed to come back to the '70's instead of the '50's? Maybe there was something just as important waiting for him in 1976. Another clue, perhaps?

Mark sighed. There were a hundred reasons. Yet the bottom line was the same. He hadn't landed in the '50's. He was in 1976 and he was more sure than not that it was a simple matter of messing up. He hadn't played correctly, the frequency was off—something had kept him from reaching his goal.

He took another sip of his cola. There was nothing he could do about it for the moment. He was too weak to travel again. He'd have to rest his body; Jessica had warned him about it. It reassured him that his fainting scene had been normal.

At least he'd met somebody friendly because of it. Barrie Chase seemed like a nice person, a little crazy and—what was the word Herbie used?—defensive? Still, she had helped him. Maybe she'd even find him something to do for the few days he'd have to spend here. At least it would keep suspicion away from him.

He stood up and headed for the door. He was amazed that the McDonald's looked exactly the way it did in '96. Same colors, same food. Except the prices. Boy, were they low!

He strolled outside. It was a sunny day in Philadelphia in 1976. He had some free time until Barrie returned with the news about the job. Maybe he'd do a little exploring. At least there were no Special Forces Agents on his trail in 1976.

Or so he thought.

"Now let me get this straight, Barrie. You want me to hire some clown refugee from a motorcycle movie to carry the kids at the mall opening? Is that what you're asking me to do?"

"Bill, you have to see this guy. He—he isn't an actor. There is nothing of the '70's about him. Or the '60's. He's so different. I don't know if he's for real '50's or not. Who can say? I was only two years old in 1951, but Bill, he is really different. He talks like the '50's, he acts like the '50's, and behind all of it, there is something about him. Believe me, boss, the girls will see it. He's trapped, he's a fighter, he's not a performer, or a clown, as you call him, he's a tortured soul, a man seeking an all right, admittedly corny, answer. But Guts is real. A real what, that I don't know, but I'll be able to tell you by tomorrow."

"This isn't like that meditative lute player you thought was going to be a big rage?"

"No."

"Or the punk rock group that destroyed the raffle car on display at the Sam Goodie spectacular?"

"Of course not."

"Or those crazy guys who all danced in a line droning 'shu-wa, shu-wa' everytime they forgot the words?"

"Bill, give me a break!"

"Or that electric country rock and blues singer, the lush in silver, who threw a petal steel riff into every line even when he was loaded?"

"Do you want me to beg? Is that it, you want me to beg forgiveness for my past sins? I don't beg, Bill."

The man behind the desk sighed and pulled himself forward in his chair. He mopped at his forehead with a Kleenex. All right, tell the guy to come in tomorrow morning. I'll give him a listen."

"Oh, thanks, Bill."

"It has nothing to do with your 'infallible' judgment. It so happens that I sent an old rock and roll guy over to see the committee people today. If they like him, I'll need someone else to spell him. So, if your Mr. Guts is anything worth listening to, I'll sign him as the relief singer. Is that fair, Barrie?"

"Fair enough."

"I mean, is that all? I won't get a call at three this morning with you on the other end telling me what a crumb I am for not giving this jerk a better deal, or something like that?"

"Yes."

"All right. Go home and make your greaser his dinner. And do anything else you want to. Just be back here at eight to do your show. That isn't too much to ask, is it?"

"Thank you, Bill!" Barrie hurried out of the office.

The station manager looked at his program. He had only three days left to fill it, and his center performer was still a question mark. "Well, I hope this is the answer. I've never seen things get so screwed up before. We should have been doing the major television spots already, rather than the 'exciting surprise guest star' we've been doing. Oh, well, let's see what they have to say." Reaching across his desk, the man dialed the shopping center's main office's number and waited.

"Guts?" Barrie responded to the knock on her door. As she walked toward it, she heard him answer from the other side. Opening it on the chain, she checked just to make sure.

"Oh, it is you." She closed the door over and slipped the latch. "Come on in. I have great news for you."

"Yeah? What's up?"

"I talked to my boss, and he wants to see you first thing in the morning."

"All right. Thank you, Barrie."

"You really sound excited."

"All he wants to do is see me. I don't have no job yet."

"Well, you could still be more excited."

Mark and Barrie continued to discuss music as they finished their dinner, then they went into the tiny living room and continued their '50's trivia conversation from the afternoon. Mark was still quite sharp. But he was far from an expert or authority.

At 7:00, she looked at her watch and stood up. "Guts, I'd love to play Twenty Questions all night, but I have to get jumping. Can't be late, you know."

"Sure, it's cool."

Barrie pulled a blanket and a pillow from her hall closet. "You can make up the couch. I won't be in 'til two-thirty, maybe three. I'll try not to wake you." Before Mark could say anything, Barrie had her purse and was headed for the door. "There's an extra set of keys in the top desk drawer, if you want to go out for a while."

"Hey, Barrie," interrupted Mark, "you're just going to leave me here?"

"Sure."

"But I could be a ripper. I could clean this joint out while you're gone."

Barrie turned in the doorway. "A ripper? You mean a thief? No, you couldn't. Not with a face like that!" She pinched the left side of Mark's chin. "Besides, you're gonna make my boss happy tomorrow. That means I have an investment to protect."

He stood looking at her, feeling suddenly shy.

Barrie smiled. "I'll see you later."

"What'll I do here all night by myself?"

"Watch TV."

Mark thought about her suggestion for a moment. Thinking of what television would become in his day, he decided against it. He also decided against going out. Jessica had given him twenty dollars in old money. It was all he had for emergencies. Deducting lunch, he did not really have any he could spare. Besides, less I mingle, less chance there is of somebody noticing something weird about me, he thought.

It was then Mark spotted the book shelves. Although he was not an avid reader—typical Mega, Herbie would say—he felt he might like to have a look. Scanning the first two rows of books, he did not find anything which caught his eye. On the third shelf he came across several volumes by H. G. Wells. He pulled one from the shelf, chuckling as he did. "*The Time Machine*, huh? Well, it'd be kind of interesting to see how somebody else did it."

Hours later, he fell asleep—dreaming of Jessica, his parents, and a bald-headed agent named Munroe.

The next morning Barrie drove Mark to the station where she worked. It was a quiet drive. Barrie was not used to getting out of bed anywhere before 2:00 or 3:00 in the afternoon at the earliest. She moaned, "People really do this? I mean, every morning?"

"Sure," answered Mark. "I used to get up at seven every morning to. . . ."

"Please." Barrie rubbed her eyes. The early morning sunlight was giving her a headache. "Don't tell me about it. Let each horror burst open me as a new experience. DJ's are not supposed to see daylight."

Mark laughed at Barrie's exaggeration. She quipped, "Do all greasers laugh at innocent people in torment?"

"I guess so."

"I'll bet you pulled the wings off flies as a kid."

Mark laughed again.

Barrie smirked. "I knew it. Under those good looks and sweet face, there's a sadist. Just my luck." Before Mark could say anything back, Barrie pulled up to the curb. "Well, I guess I have some good luck, anyway. A parking spot only a half block from the building."

"Is that good?"

"In this city? It ain't bad. Come on, handsome. Get your guitar from the back seat and let's go."

They entered the radio station building on Philadelphia's trendy Main Line. Mark followed Barrie to her boss's office. It was empty.

"He just stepped out," said a secretary. "Bill will be back in a minute. He's always running all over the place."

True to the woman's prediction, the station manager came in a few minutes later. Very tall, sporting twenty pounds too many, he barged into his office, waving his cigar in a circular motion. "I said 'in the *morning*,' Chase. It's almost noon. The committee people got here an hour ago. I thought I'd have time to hear this croaker before they got here at least." The man took Mark's hand. "Hi, Bill Grogen, you're the kid, right?" Mark nodded. "Right, 'course you are, who else would you be? All right, kid, I hope you're good. They approved this old rock and roller yesterday. Now all I need is something to round him out. I told them you were probably it. They're expecting a lot. Can you deliver?"

The man didn't wait for an answer. "Ah, sure you can. Let's get down there. C'mon, let's go. You'll knock their socks off." He glanced at Mark with a mixture of friendship and menace. "Won't you?"

"Just as sure as you'll get my bill in the morning."

"Hey, this kid's got a brain," said Grogen. "Maybe you finally found somebody legit, Barrie. About time, that's all I can say."

Barrie shoved away the cigar Grogen was waving in her face. Grogen looked at Mark. "What was your name again?"

"Guts, man. Just call me Guts."

"Glad to meet you, Gutsman. Now let's get going. We got sponsors to impress."

"I'll bring him down in a second," Barrie said. "You can hurry ahead of us."

"They're waiting in the studio. I'll let them know you're on the way. Ahhh, this'll take care of our problems." The man hurried out through his office door, trailing cigar ashes behind him. Mark let out a sigh.

"He's hot-wired, isn't he?"

"Bill's a nice man," Barrie answered. "He runs a good station. He's just tense."

Mark nodded and picked up his guitar.

"Don't you have a case for that thing?"

"Nope. Couldn't see the point. When my fingers want to play, they don't want anything to stop 'em. Not even for a second."

"I'll take your word for it. We'd better get moving now. This could be a big chance for you, Guts. You could really start a little career rolling for yourself, you know. That is, if you can play; I mean, really play well."

"I can. I even do."

Barrie held the door open for Mark. He went into the outer office and then to the studio. Once in the studio, he looked over the three committee members. "Well, they don't look too mean," he whispered to Barrie, "but then again, they haven't liked all that much so far."

Barrie whispered back, "Guts, I haven't even heard you play. Do you realize that? I don't even know for sure if you know which end of a guitar is which. But I brought you here anyway. Do you know why?"

Mark smiled. "Why's that, honey?"

She squeezed his hand. "I'm self-destructive, that's why. You better sing as good as you talk, Guts. Think you can do it? Now is the time to show your stuff."

Mark faced the committee members. He walked the few steps to the microphone positioned in the center of a weak spotlight. He said softly, "Good morning. I'm sorry I'm late. Actually, we didn't know we had an appointment, but let's leave the excuses for later. Right now, I guess I'd better get down to the program. My name is Guts. I'd like to do an old number for you that was written by David Star; it's called, 'Cause You're Not Here.' "

Mark plugged his guitar into the amplifier next to the microphone. There was no feedback. His hands moved across the strings and played the three-chord intro to the lonely song. He kept his fingers moving, gently pulling the soft melody

138

along, teasing his audience with the quiet notes. Then, once he had brought them to the edge, he sang.

Nobody was sure who started applauding first. The committee members, Barrie, Grogen, the several scattered technicians; everyone had planned to politely clap and then let Mark get on to his next number. He had to wait longer than he had expected.

"Is he everything I said, huh?"

"He's splendid, Mr. Grogen. He knows the song as well as Star himself. He'll be perfect."

"I have to agree, Grogen. This Guts of yours is fine. Start whatever last minute publicity you can."

"Come to my office. Let's get the final papers all drawn. Yes, indeed."

Grogen ushered the shopping center committee out of the studio. Mark was dumbstruck. He had thought he would have to do eight, nine, maybe ten different numbers before they would reach a decision. He was amazed that everything was over so quickly. He asked Barrie, "That's it? That's all it takes?"

"All it takes is you, I guess." The woman threw her arms around Mark. "Guts, you really made that song come alive. I never heard it done that way, I mean, except by Star. It's such a simple tune—most people won't even try it because it's so hard to get the feeling. But how did you know to do a Star number?"

"I know a lot of his stuff. What'd you mean?"

"About what?"

"You said, 'How'd I know to play a Star number?' What'd you mean?"

"Don't you know?"

"Would I be askin'?"

"I'm sorry. I thought you overheard somebody talking. The man on the bill with you, at the shopping mall, is David Star."

Mark sat in Barrie's apartment. She was working; he was waiting. He had been thinking of attempting another jump, trying to make it back to 1956 before meeting Star. He did feel strong enough. The first trip had been more draining than he thought. "Damn," he thought. "I knew there had to be something, some reason why I stopped here instead of going further back. I was supposed to meet Star here. It has to be."

The more Mark thought about it, however, the less sense his idea made. "But how would he know I was coming? How would I find him? Getting this job wasn't part of his plans, no matter how clever Star and Herbie were, they couldn't have planned something like that." Mark scratched his head. He had asked Barrie to get in touch with Star for him. She had tried, but she couldn't find him. Star had a show to do in Pittsburgh. Mark would not be able to see him until Sunday.

Mark was puzzled. He didn't know a lot of things about time travel. Did a person remember things that happened with somebody from another time? If Star had met Herbie in the '50's when Herbie had gone back to hide the BCS secrets, would Star remember him now in 1976? Or would the memory disappear?

Maybe the log book would have a clue. He pulled it out of his jacket. Should he take a chance on seeing Star now? Would Star remember that he had met him in the future? Throwing the jacket over the arm of his chair, he leaned back and again began looking through the pages of figures. It was all meaningless to him.

The pages seemed to be listings of records and nothing else. Only the back page, with its simple code had another meaning to him. Mark wished he could find the key which would solve its mystery. He wanted to go back to Jess and Manny with the answers, and the evidence. He wanted to see his parents again. He wanted to see Mega, to find out what happened to Herbie. He took the record out of the log book and looked at it again. He had a clue. He knew it had to be a clue—he had to figure it out.

A few hours later, Barrie came in quietly. She assumed Mark would be asleep and did not want to disturb him. She was correct. Tiptoeing, she went to her bedroom. On the way to her bathroom later, she watched Mark sleeping. Somehow, not talking in his continual '50's monologue, he seemed much younger to her. His head was against the arm of the chair. He was sleeping with his mouth open, snoring slightly. She tried to picture him as the man who had sung in the studio the day before. She had trouble doing so. Asleep, with his face uncreased, the worry lines gone from his forehead, Mark seemed too young, too innocent to have sung the lonely song the way he had.

"What could have made you so lonely, so soon?" she wondered. "What are you running from, Guts? What do you want?" Barrie stepped into her room and shut the door. She slipped between her sheets, still thinking about Mark. Everyone under the age of twenty was looking for something, she mused, but Mark was driven. There was something guarded in the way he talked to people, even her. Barrie was determined to find out why Mark was so secretive. She knew there was something important about the log book, and something even more important about the old David Star record in it. There was some connection between Mark and Star.

CHAPTER ELEVEN

It was Sunday afternoon. Barrie and Mark were having lunch. "Are you awake yet, Barrie?"

The woman nodded and groaned. "Yes. I think so. Give me a few more hours. Maybe I'll open my eyes the whole way." Mark laughed.

"I'm goin' out for a while."

"Anywhere in particular?"

"No, just want to catch the view, see the sights. Tonight's my big night, you know."

"Just be back in time."

"I'll meet you out at the shopping center."

"Guts!"

"Don't worry. I'll be there. I know where it is. I know when it is. And most important, I need the green, so I'll be there. No sweat."

As Mark went for his jacket, Barrie said, "I noticed you've been doing some reading."

"A little."

"I didn't know greasers knew how to read."

He smiled back at her. "A little."

"Find anything you like?"

"I did read one that I wanted to ask you about."

"Ask away."

Mark sat back down. He said, "That time machine book. I've been thinking about it. You remember the Morlocks. Wouldn't you say that they were in charge?"

"They were running things."

"They controlled things, didn't they? The Eloi didn't even know they were being manipulated; they would just hear a sound and go get eaten."

"So what's the question?"

"Do you think that could happen today? People being controlled by something like that without knowing it?"

Barrie looked up at him. She put her sandwich back on its plate. She finished chewing and said, "According to some sources, we just got rid of that problem." Mark looked at her, not speaking.

"You know. Nixon." She smiled.

Mark did not understand her.

He answered, "Seriously. Do you think it could really happen like that? I mean the government and big business with money and clout, controlling everybody without their knowing it?"

"I don't think so, but I do know something else."

"What's that?"

"When you get serious, you don't talk like a greaser."

Mark was shocked. He stayed silent for a second, and then answered, "Well, yeah. You know. Can't act all the time. It's good for the image and all, but sometimes things can slip. But don't worry, I'll be '50's tonight."

Before Barrie could continue, Mark had already picked up the log book and slid it into his jacket pocket. "I'll see you at the shopping center tonight. You're going to be there, aren't you?"

"Yes, but, Guts. . . ."

"Hey, I got to get out. I got to cruise a little. Been cooped up too long. I'll see you tonight."

Barrie sat down. She knew she would never learn the truth about Mark. Something told her, an intuition. She did not understand. Mark was not just using her, she was positive. She was also sure she would never know his secret. As he headed for the door, she waved her fingers at him. "Bye. I'll see you tonight."

"See ya. You're gonna bring my guitar out tonight, right?"

She smiled affectionately, but did not reply. Mark closed the door behind him. Barrie watched it. After a while, she stood up. She hoped she could reach Grogen in time. He would have to take the guitar to the shopping center for Mark. She wouldn't be going. She folded Mark's blanket and sheet, and took them with the pillow he had been using back to the closet. Somehow she knew he would have no further use for them.

Mark walked along the streets of Philadelphia, taking in the sights of 1976. He wondered about some of the theories Jessica had told him about time. David Star had explained that as long as a person wasn't in two places at once, history would be unaffected. If a person did attempt to be in two places at once, the later person would immediately die. In effect, a person could not exist in two places at once. If the theory were correct, he would not come back to this time and place again. To take his mind off things, Mark browsed through the shops, the book and record stores in Philadelphia's Center City. He thumbed through comic books and film magazines. None of the names he had memorized appeared. Many rock and roll performers, movie stars, some of the personalities so important in the '50's were gone. Some of the biggest, most unforgettable names in the business showed up in small, minor nostalgia pieces. A few were still important. Some seemed to have disappeared completely, like they'd never been there in the first place.

Mark continued down the street. The log book had become a permanent fixture, jutting into his waist uncomfortably, as if it were nagging him to open it again. He wished there was some other way to get an answer from it—but if Jessica couldn't figure out what to do with the record in the future, how could he possibly find out anything more in the past?

Unless—he smiled—there were things they knew now that had been forgotten later! Sure—he reached for the log book— Herbie was always teaching him things that had been forgotten! Just because he came from the future, it didn't mean they knew more—they just knew different things!

He ran down the street toward an old wooden sign that said "Records: New—Old—Used."

Once inside, he looked around the high-ceilinged room. It was stacked with old albums and singles. It reminded him of Herbie's room.

A friendly man was watching him from behind a glass counter that faced the front door.

"Can I help you with something, young man?"

"I sure hope so. You got anyone who really knows about records here? I don't mean singers or bands or anything, I mean about the way records are made, stuff like that."

"I'm fairly familiar with records. What seems to be your problem?"

"Well, I have this old record, see. I have this friend who's always smartin' off, you know? Well, anyway, he looks this record of mine over, and he says, 'Hey, Mark. This record of yours. It's different.' And when I ask him what he's talkin' about, he clams up on me and don't tell me nuthin'. So far, *nobody's* been able to figure out what he's talkin' about, right? I'm hopin' maybe you can spot somethin' about it? What'd ya say, man?"

The older man answered, "Well, I'll certainly take a look at it. I assume you've played it."

"Oh yeah, every speed. Everything." Mark handed the man the 45. The clerk took it, handling it carefully.

"Did you put the tape on these labels?"

"Yeah. I thought there might be something underneath, you know? So I soaked them off with hot water. There wasn't nuthin' though, so I taped 'em back on."

The clerk nodded and continued to study the record. He "um-hummed" a few times, but said nothing directly to Mark. He turned the record over, held it to the light, and then suddenly, he smiled.

Mark asked, "You find somethin'?"

"I think I may have! Look here! You see these two letters and then a number. That identifies the company. 'PH' stands for 'Phillies Records.' The number next to it is the number assigned to this specific record title."

Mark was disappointed. "I know that, sir. All records have them."

The man looked at Mark. "Exactly! Then you should *also* know that there is always one number and one set of letters on each record. Not two!"

"Two?" Mark reached for the record.

"Look at this!" The man held the record up next to the light. "Right next to Spector's number is another—*HB 2011.* I never heard of any HB series coding on a Phillies release."

Mark took the record. "HB 2011," he whispered. "HB 2011. HB—Herbie Bender!"

"I'll give you twenty-five dollars for the. . . ."

Mark was already on his way outside the store. "Thanks!" he shouted. "Thanks a lot!"

Returning to the street, he spotted an electric clock atop one of the larger buildings. It was time for him to head toward the shopping center.

As he rode in a taxi toward the address Barrie had told him, he stared at the numbers. HB—that was Herbie for sure—but what did 2011 mean? Was it an address or a locker number or another of Herbie's codes?

"If it's a code like in the back of the log book, then each number stands for a letter. 2011. B is the second letter of the alphabet. But there isn't any zero—unless A is zero and B is one. That would make C the number two. 2011=CABB. CABB? That doesn't make too much sense. It could be something else, like the number of a license plate or the number of a telephone or. . . ."

"No, telephone numbers have seven numbers—HB 2011 would only be six. What has four numbers and means something?"

Mark smiled. He had been traveling time long enough to have figured out the obvious first. "A year! Of course! *2011* could mean a year!"

The cab hopped a freshly paved curve and rolled up to the edge of a parking lot.

"Too much traffic back there. Some sort of opening going on in front of the stores." The woman behind the wheel turned to Mark. "That'll be six seventy-five."

Mark gulped and paid the bill.

As the cabbie took off, he observed the scene. Although it was early—the show would not start for half an hour—kids were already filling up the area around the grandstand. He headed through the cars toward the outdoor stage.

As he reached the front of the growing audience, Mark looked around for Barrie. He did not see her or her car. He saw someone strumming his guitar on stage, testing the mikes.

Before he could walk around the stage, though, he heard a familiar voice. "Hey, Guts. Guts, boy. Over here. Let's get this show on the road."

"Mr. Grogen."

"Yes, sir. I've been waiting for you. So has Star. Wants to meet you."

"Star. He's here?"

"Well of course he's here. C'mon now. I figure you two want to do a little talking. Pull some sort of a show together. This has been the most confused thing I've ever done. C'mon around back. I got your guitar back there."

"You have it? Where's Barrie?"

"Don't worry about it. You know Barrie—always runnin'. C'mon, Star'll be waiting in back."

Mark followed the station manager back behind the stage. Sitting on a folding metal chair, plucking a nonsense tune on his guitar, was David Star. He had just walked off stage.

"David, I'd like you to meet Mark Gutstein."

"You're my opening act, eh? Welcome to Philly."

Mark smiled and shook Star's hand. He looked at him very closely, surprised to see the singer's youthful vitality. The David Star he knew was the man this Star would become—a weary but sagacious hero.

Grogen patted both men on the back.

"Yes sir, Mr. Star. This kid does your stuff to where it would make you cry. You two will work fine."

Star looked at Mark.

"Sorry I couldn't be here to work with you a couple of days. Let's work out a little bit of fun, okay, Guts?"

Mark nodded. It was maddening! David Star didn't seem to know a thing about him. Or did he? Had Herbie contacted this David Star to tell him about the trouble he'd have in the future. Was Star keeping silent in front of Grogen? Mark watched the station manager take care of last-minute back-stage preparations.

"Grogen's a hard worker," Mark said to Star. "I ain't got no beef with th' way he's handlin' me. You?"

Star stared at him. "What are you saying, kid?"

"Grogan's cool, huh, man?"

Star started to laugh. "You're putting me on, aren't you? Makin' fun of my 'roots,' huh?"

Mark shook his head. "Don't know what you mean."

Star analyzed the young man. He was nineteen, nervous, obviously sensitive, and hiding something. "You're a fake," he said as a challenge. "I don't play with fakes. Come clear with me or I'll tell Grogen to take you off the bill."

Mark almost dropped his guitar. He needed Star for a friend. His '50's act was threatening that friendship before it had even started. What could he do? Either Star knew who he was now or he knew nothing at all. If he didn't know anything, then Mark couldn't tell him. Jessica had taught him never to say anything about the future to a person in the past.

"I'm sorry," Mark replied quickly, "it's just the way I like to talk."

Star nodded. "Just don't push it around me. I'm a good person to play with, Mark, and if I like you I may be able to use you on tour. Despite what you may have heard, I still play regular gigs."

"I know," Mark answered. "I think you're one of the best."

Star smiled. "Thanks. Now let's see what you can do."

"Gutstein! In five!"

Mark looked up at center stage and saw Grogan walking toward a mike. Although the crowd was not yet full, the concert was about to start.

"Men and Women! Boys and Girls! I'm Bill Grogen, Station manager of WFUN and. . . ."

"Where's Barrie?" said a boy in the crowd.

"We want Barrie!" said another.

"Barrie is unable to make it for personal reasons, but. . . ."

"Boo!"

"Bring back Barrie!"

Grogan reddened. *"All right now! Barrie will be on her regular time on WFUN. Right now we have a special treat for you—the best of the old and the best of the new—two fantastic singer-guitarists from Philly are to greet the opening of the new Ben Franklin shopping center!"*

There was a clapping from the store owner's children up front.

"Now here's one of the most exciting new talents I've had the privilege to hear in years! I want a big welcome for—GUTS!"

Star smiled, "Rock on, kid!"

Mark ran toward the steps of the stage, and kept running. As he reached the mike, Grogan quickly headed off stage and Mark launched into one of the songs that Manny had taught him. It was called "Heartbreak Hotel."

Mark did not look at the crowd until he was a minute into the song. They were quiet, he thought, so they either loved him or had already left.

He speeded up into a fast bridge and glanced out in the crowd. Young mostly, and attentive. Good. In the back there were a few older people, listening less attentively but still....

He eyed a bald man in a hat about twenty yards away. Funny, he looked just like the man who had chased him through Mega-20. He looked just like *Munroe.*

Then Mark launched into another stanza of "Heartbreak Hotel."

Too many coincidences, he thought. First Star, then a man who looks like Munroe. He looked again. The bald-headed man was walking through the crowd toward the stage.

Mark gasped. It wasn't a man who resembled Munroe. It *was* Munroe! The Special Forces captain was here, in Philly! In 1976!

He put his back to the stage and kept singing. As he did, he motioned backstage to David Star.

Star saw the kid waving up on the stage. It was far too soon. The kid was supposed to do three numbers! He wasn't even through with the first. Nonetheless, he hurried up to find out what he wanted.

As Mark concluded "Hearbreak Hotel," Star reached the mike, guitar in hand. Mark approached him. *"Ladies and gentlemen..."*

Off stage, Grogan was tinting a lovely shade of red. "What's that kid doing! Not another looney! Not again!"

"... This man is a rock and roll legend. I am so proud to be here with him today, that I've asked him up on stage to join me in playing one of his most famous numbers—'Time to be Good.'"

Grogan leaned against his engineer. "Oy. Get me a chair, will ya?"

"Ladies and gentlemen—David Star!"

There were hoots and applause. Mark strummed the opening chords of "Time To Be Good." He hadn't learned the whole song by memory and was depending on Star to cover. He only hoped there'd be time to enact his plan.

As Star picked up the song, Mark whispered to him, "I know this is going to sound crazy, but there's somebody out there who wants to kill you."

Star glared at him.

"I know, I know. It sounds crazy. Who would want to kill you? Don't think about it. Just cover for me!"

Mark spun around again and kept his back to the stage. Reaching into his pocket, he pulled out the safety pouch in which the electromagnetic amplifier bars had been kept. Concentrating, he put them in his palm, ripped open his shirt, and held them in front of his chest.

In front of him, a puzzled David Star went into a chorus of *"There's always time to be good."*

Mark faced the audience again. He searched out Munroe. The man had come within close proximity of the stage. He could see him, could see him looking at him. If Munroe spotted the bars, it would be clear to him what Mark was about to do.

Mark stood next to Star and resumed playing.

"Come on, baby, sing my rhyme.
    I just know you could,
    I just know that you should.
Come on, my sweetheart,
    There's always time to be good."

Mark slid a electronic key at the base of his guitar. There was a humming sound and Star looked up suspiciously.

"Keep playing!" Mark whispered.

He looked out in the crowd and Munroe was reaching into his jacket pocket.

"Come on, my sweetheart, there. . ."

The fading started, the humming grew, Mark strummed faster, harder, wider, fuller, and then grabbed hold of Star's jacket.

"What are. . . ?"

Star started to pull away from Mark, but it was too late.

"What's happening to. . . ?"

Mark took a deep breath and said, "Hang on, Mr. Star, we're going to take a little journey!"

In the next ten seconds, Mark Gutstein and David Star vanished from the stage.

Munroe watched in frustration.

The kid was going—gone! After all they'd done—after the trackdown, the round-up. It was a mad game with too many pieces in play.

Bender had escaped. Star was still missing. They had disappeared again! They had the lab, but the key figures had all eluded the Special Forces men.

Floating through time, Mark Gutstein faced David Star. The man was in shock. He himself was fainting fast. He had not wanted to travel again as quickly as he had, but it had seemed to be the safest, fastest way to escape.

He did not know where he was headed. He had set the guitar without planning, and he had used the bars as quickly as possible to protect himself It was risky taking Star, but his guess was that Munroe had been sent to get rid of Star in the past. That meant the secret of time travel was out.

He watched the black capsules floating in time ahead of him. He was floating slower this time, he knew it. As the capsules came closer to him, he thought one of the smaller capsules was floating out of its trajectory in his direction.

After a few seconds (minutes? years?), he realized it was. It approached closer, and as it did, it started to open.

The closer it came, the slower he floated. He looked at Star.

The singer was unconscious.

Mark felt himself being drawn closer and closer to the open capsule. He gripped Star tightly—if he could do anything, it would be to help Star first.

The capsule rotated softly in front of them. Mark peered inside and saw little more than a shiny blackness. He attempted to pull away from it, but the capsule floated under him. Moments later he was inside it. Trapped in a silent prison with David Star. Unable to move, unable to scream, Mark waited.

Then, suddenly, as the capsule closed above them, they heard a sound. A voice. It was deep, and faded, but familiar. Mark knew it, he'd know it anywhere.

"Do not move," it said. *"You are safe. You are headed toward Binary Rescue Station Six. Welcome back, Guts."*

The voice belonged to Herbie Bender.

NEXT: In *Guts, Book Two*, Mark finds Herbie Bender, and the fantastic adventures of David Star continue. WOW!!!

www.ingramcontent.com/pod-product-compliance
Lightning Source LLC
Chambersburg PA
CBHW070037260626
47159CB00005B/2063